ON THE TRAIL WITH CISCO PEACH

S. Southcott

This is a work of fiction. All characters and events portrayed in this book are either products of the author's imagination or are used fictitiously.

ON THE TRAIL WITH CISCO PEACH

A Star Brand Dime Novel
Star Brand Publications

ISBN 978-0-6152-1632-4

Printed in the United States of America

Acknowledgments

I thank the Good Lord for giving me a rock to stand on when I was tired of jumping in the mud.

I thank my family for humoring me when I give them random Western History facts, especially my husband Charles who has been a complete gem.

Thank you Paul for giving me a place to work and be myself.

Thank you VJ for telling me I could do it.

Jen, there is no way I could have done this without you, my partna in editing crime.

Introduction

I have had a long-standing love affair with the West. I grew up with Roy Rogers, Bonanza, and Gunsmoke. I shot guns and collected Breyer horse models instead of playing with dolls. Being born a girl was definitely a hindrance since all the cool heroes were men.

I found out later that the actual West did include female heroes as well as a tapestry of other colorful characters that just don't get into "print." For instance, I read that one in three cowboys were of African American or Hispanic origin. Where are their stories? Women were definitely involved in rodeo as bull and bronc riders up until the early 1900's. This last bit of information could have been invaluable to me as an incurable tomboy! Asian immigrants traveled to the "Gold Mountain" and built a railroad and their fortunes with their hard work ethic.

I tried my best to give a hats off to those who weren't wearing the white hats in the movies. This includes the American Indian to which I have tried to show the utmost respect for in this story.

This one is for Pearl, The little "Lady Bandit" with a big story.

"From reckless despair, she drifted into the life; it is with determination bordering on reckless that she starts to quit it."

-Josie Washburn, Madam

"Therefore I tell you, her many sins have been forgiven-for she loved much. But he who has been forgiven little loves little."

-Jesus

1

My eyes were bugged out and my face was red. I was sure of it even though I couldn't see it. My jaw was working furiously to hold back the swelling in my throat; which at the moment was directly under his clenched fist. I didn't make it any easier that my feet were danglin' about six inches above the floor boards. His stinky breath was a cloud over my plans for an escape. I looked Ma's way, there was no help there. I guess survival reflexes kicked in, cuz so did my knee. I hit him in a tender spot, and he let go of his tight grip and cussed up a storm. My feet were runnin' before they even hit the floor, taking the rest of me with um out the door and for the hills. He finally passed out later that night.

*

The start of the trail for me was a rough one. Ma, Pa and me had a small homestead on the prairie with lots of rough work day-in and day-out. The land was unforgiving, either scorchin' hot or bitin' cold. There was a constant wind that left you with sandpaper eyes, leather skin, and broke up lips. There was sagebrush and long-eared rabbits, lizards, snakes, and coyotes. We cracked the ground every spring to try and bring some kind life to our little patch of land. My favorite part of day was sunset; with its reds, yellows, and purples. I would stop and watch the sun set from anywhere I was at the time. It was the kind of place that made you either tough or dead; maybe even both in the end.

Ma was raised in a fine Christian-type home that believed that a woman should be taught to read and write; then shut her mouth. Especially when it came to the affairs of men, which is what probably set her up for marrying the wrong man. She was lead to believe he was the fine Christian-type himself, not the hard-drinkin', woman-beatin', no-workin' type he turned out to be. She shut her mouth one too many times if you ask me. Then again, she did the best she could. Of course, I was a disappointment to the man who was outspoken about the fact that I was not born a boy. What made matters worse was that during my delivery, there was enough damage to make sure that there would be no more children for them, much less a son. It was me who became the designated "son".

Life for me was an endless list of chores. Diggin' this, haulin' that, repairin' something else, caring for sick or hurt animals, and everything in between. A lot of it was work for a man, but he slept a lot. I suppose that when he rode off in the evenings he wound up back here, tired of the sporting houses with their gambling and alcohol. He came riding back to this place of disappointment on the Red. The Red was a beaut of a tall blood-brown stallion that he won in a card game with a rich Southern man. If you ask me, The Red got the raw end of the deal. This accounted for the fact that nobody could get near the animal without a fight. I suppose he kept the horse for braggin' rights alone. There was no finer animal anywhere in our piece of the world.

During the times he was away Ma and I would sit together. She would teach me about reading and writing and numbers. She was an expert card player; poker and hearts were her favorites. How that happened was always a mystery to me, considering how she grew up. I wasn't about to question her on it cuz I was surely becoming an expert myself. I didn't want her to quit on me while I was ahead of the game, so to speak.

One rare occasion Pa called me over. He held a pistol in his hand. I just figured my time was up. To my surprise he shoved it in my hand and showed me how to shoot some cans off the fence. The repeated slap to the head for missing didn't seem too bad after a while. The feeling I got holdin' that gun was worth every one of um. Besides, I started to get good. I practiced every chance I got, and then some. I even snuck far up into the mountains when he was asleep. If he woke and found me gone, that would have meant more than a slap for sure. I shot at everything I could see, movin' or not. You see for me, this was the one thing I could have control of. The fact was the better shot in a fight would win out over quick and fancy draws that missed. Quick didn't matter when you were dead. I found out to my surprise that I could hit most anything, not just with one hand but with both.

*

Birthdays weren't usually celebrated around our place, but I think it was around my 14 or 15 year that certain events occurred that would change my life forever.

Hiding places were a way of life for me. There were attic places, barn places, mountain brush places, and places in my head that I ran to when things got bad. It was the attic place that surprised me most of all one night. It had been a long day and I was done. Done with the work. Done with all the yelling and screaming in our house. Done with life in general. Someone caught on, cuz when I hid in the attic; I found a note attached to the old trunk with my name on it. Inside the old trunk I found my ticket out.

My ticket out was a full set of men's clothes, a small pouch of coins, cutting shears, and two colt pistols with a hand-tooled holster. Some folks said that, "God made men, but Sam Colt made um equal." Well, in my case, I had begun to believe just that. Only, it made this girl just as equal, with better than average aim, and a whole lot of anger behind the trigger. Being naturally flat-chested only helped the final outcome of my outfit. Just to be safe, I tore my old shirt into strips and wrapped um around my chest as tight as I could. I began to shear my hair off as close as I could to my head. Every lock of hair that fell to the floor boards felt a little more like freedom.

I headed toward the barn with one thought running through my head.

"Time to spring The Red."

I figured I couldn't come out of this without a fight. I was thinkin' that The Red needed freedom as much as I did right about now. I was aiming toward the barn with those thoughts banging 'round in my head.

2

Scared wasn't even the word, but there was no time. I don't even remember how I got that saddle on. I wrapped a handful of thick mane around my glove and kicked. There was wood- splittin', dust kickin', barn door-breakin' chaos. As I swung by the house, I saw my ma in the window for the last time. She had her hand on the window, fingers spread in a goodbye wave. My house was in flames. I hadn't even smelled the smoke. I figured that she knew I was leaving somehow and didn't want to carry on with that man alone. I had no time to sort it all out.

There was no stopping that crazy red devil of a horse. All night I rode, and into the next morning light. I could see that the part of my hand that was wrapped in the horse's mane was also covered in blood. My body ached from the cold and the long ride. Funny thing was, I hadn't even shed a tear, but my head felt like it had been pounded with a hammer from the inside out. Every time a hoof hit the ground, it sent pain from my backside to my brain. As I rode on I thought it would never end. It was as if the red devil was running back to hell with me along for the ride. I wondered if hell was any worse than the burning place I left behind.

It was the creek that came up and grabbed that horse. He stopped so fast that I was yanked to the ground by the force of it all. Early spring grass cushioned my fall. It didn't seem to help ease the pain in my body, especially in my mangled hand.

*

I was afraid to look under that bloody glove. Out on the prairie with an injury and havin' no food, water, or shelter could mean death for some. I only had water so far.

The Red and I both drank from the creek. While I was figuring how to get across the swelled creek, the horse made up my mind for me. To this day, I never seen a horse jump into the water like he did that day. He must've been just as done as I was with what we left behind. There wasn't but one thing to do. I jumped in right behind, holding onto the horn with all my might. There was pain shooting through my hurt hand as I tried to keep my guns above water. We both came out wet and runnin' again.

The ice cold water cooled the pain in my head and my hand a bit. I reached up with my arm and wiped my forehead with my shirt sleeve as the wind went whippin' bye. We rode along until I saw a silver ribbon of smoke coming up from behind the hill in the morning light. The Red caught one whiff of that smoke, stopped short, and started backing up. I had to tie him up and sneak over to get a closer look at what we were coming up on. You can never be too careful when it comes to strangers. There were folks who would kill ya for little else than a wrong look, or the gear on your saddle.

I saw a run-down cabin with three horses tied outside. One brown, one grey, and one spotted with a Indian blanket and saddle. That made my mind whirl. Why would an Indian pony be anywhere near to the others? From what I could figure, alcohol was involved. I could hear loud voices and the sound of breakin' glass. I knew that sound. I gripped my gun so tight that my bloody hand throbbed, white knuckles and all.

*

Squeezing one eye ball through a knot hole in a board, I could see two men fighting and what looked like an Indian girl. She was tied up by her hands and ankles in the corner of the room, with a rag stuffed in her mouth. She didn't look panicked, just like she was waiting for her chance to get away. I knew how she felt. Her eyes were wide open, studying the room, and watching the two men fighting. They were dirty, unshaven, and sloppy drunk. I caught the tail end of their conversation.

"Why didn't you just take the horse instead of that there Talk'in Book no good squaw?!"

One of the men threw an empty bottle her way, which crashed against the wall right above her head. She didn't even flinch. She just stared straight ahead and held her chin up. This seemed to strike a nerve with the men, cuz they started toward her with clenched fists. I was done watching.

A deadly anger grew inside me. Heat mixed with a buzzing sound in my ears. Angry buzzing bees. That noise made kicking in the door easy work. The place was fallin' down as it was. I heard the shots that left two men dead. It was like someone else pulled the trigger. I was surprised to find that I felt nothing. Like the heart in my chest had long been choked off and backed into a cold dark place, a hiding place. The heat and the buzzing were gone. Just quiet and a sort of emptiness was left.

I noticed a pair of eyes locked on me, waiting. I holstered my guns and slowly held out my hand to her. She studied it, her black eyebrows coming up slightly when she saw the blood. I studied her. She was about my age, maybe a bit older. It was those eyes, almost black with a little light behind them, like the sun coming up over the hilltop. She had long black lashes, waving like wings of a great black bird. Her skin was like polished leather, with a manner to match. She stayed by my side, and remained there after we left that place of death. Those men, along with a part of my soul stayed there that day. We cut the other horses loose and rode off.

Some folks say bad things about the Indians. In my lifetime, I have never found a truer and more loyal friend than Talking Book.

3

Some might say that life on the trail is a free and easy one. That is until you lived it awhile yourself. Here we were, on the trail for about a year. My hand long since healed thanks to a little help from my new riding partner. It seems that pains of the heart take a bit longer to heal. I wish I could wrap up the feeling's inside with healing herbs and cloth and be shut of the past. But it ain't that easy.

Talking Book had taken up my dressing style and cut her long black hair to fit under her hat. We lived like men and with men; takin' care to never let out our secret. We worked when we could find it. Sometimes we took meals from places we passed by. To our good fortune, names weren't important to most. The code of the day said that it was impolite to ask about the private affairs of strangers, during a complimentary meal or otherwise.

Our hands and skin became rough and cracked due to weather. There was always the dry wind that sucked every drop of water from our bones and left the grainy feeling of sand in our hair, eyes, and teeth. Soon our backsides became used to the daily abuse of riding; even our insides had hardened up to the natural emotions that come with being a girl. Still, we were free to come and go as we pleased.

We enjoyed star-speckled skies, and the flower-carpeted plains, with its yellows and purples. We traveled on high mountain peaks with nothing but the high calling sound of hawks and wolves, and the child-like laughter of coyotes. We breathed in the pine-scented air and listened to the wind whisper in the leaves. We ate fish and game that we caught or shot along the way. When sundown came we would sit by our little fire and dream.

In all the time we left that old cabin, Talking Book hadn't spoken one word. I learned to read her expressions though. It left me wondering if we should just take out the Talking part of her name all together and just call her Book, *Closed* Book.

*

Wrestling with The Red had become routine and usually happened at the worst of times. We rode into a town that had a gamblin' house by the name of Red Leg's Last Chance. We were tired and hungry and needed the cash. I threw back to my old habit of playing cards with a vengeance. Talking Book never came with me into gamblin' houses. That was different than most Indians who would gamble away their own wives or horses on any game of chance. I decided to not make mention of it due to the fact that she would put on a stone expression as we rode up. To make a short story of the whole mess ain't easy.

Most gamblin' houses had older, rougher men who did not take too well to a young, smooth-faced "boy" and his no-talkin' Indian friend leaving with all of their money. I had a whole table of their money, which they

11

were gonna take back by force. I could tell by the way they stood up from the table and whispered to each other. That spelt out, "time to go" in western talk, if you were smart. I headed out the door of the gamblin' house with the idea to do just that. With my eyes fixed on the door, I grabbed for the reins. The Red started backing up with a fine set of flattened ears, which spelt out, "I ain't movin" in horse talk.

Talking Book jumped down from her own spotted horse and grabbed The Red's nose with both hands. She made a "shush shush" sound, breathed into his nostrils and said in a loud, clear voice and in the most perfect English I'd ever heard.

"Peace, peace little brother!"

It was like time stood still. Something lit out of that horse and never returned. Not the speed, but the meanness. Like a rushing of wind, he breathed out a sigh of relief. She jumped back on her horse, I jumped on mine, and we were off.

4

A while out of town, I was still trying to figure what I heard. A few weeks later, she relayed her life story to me in bits and pieces. I had to wait ya see, cuz my respect for her and her ways kept me from reaching for more. It just kind of trickled out of her like a thawing spring river. Then one day it happened that I had the whole tale. I will try to recount her story for you here.

Her father was a chieftain of a local tribe who had a taste for the white man's ways of dress, and in particular, men's hair care pomade. Now, being an Indian, he wasn't much interested in the shaving products. The fact was there wasn't much hair on his face, which was the case with most Indian men. The chief would paste his shiny black hair down with pomade and put a top hat on his head like a crown with an eagle feather stuck in the side. True to his self-centered nature, he would trade for various hair products at a frenzied pace with any trader that came along, putting his tribe in danger of poverty by squandering resources.

This did not sit well with the tribe who expected their Chief to put their needs first. Tribes were often times poor and traded with furs, hand-made items, and horses in exchange for things they needed. Trading for steel tools and guns was common. For tribes, gun-power ruled the plains. Pressure from the tribe caused the Chief to come up with a plan of his own. He would send his young daughter "Talking Bird" to the homestead of some nearby settlers. She had orders to steal any men's hair care items within her tiny hands reach and report back to him quick time. Much to the dismay of the Chief, the plan didn't work out quite that way.

Indian ways are pretty set, especially where their names are concerned. Soon after the Chief's child was born, her grandmother witnessed the child and a large bird having what sounded like a regular conversation. They named her "Talking Bird". This was unusual because boys were often named after an animal or bird. The little girl lived up to her name in a big way. She sounded like an adult before long, having conversations with anyone who would listen. Now Indians were known to take a gamble now and then. The Chief took a bet on his one and only daughter. He figured she could talk her way into the house and hearts of the nearby white settlers.

What he didn't know was that these particular settlers happened to be poor missionaries. They had come to the plains to convert the Indians and were having a rough go of it because the "white man's religion" was hard for the Indian people to accept. It cut them off from their people, making them outcasts between their world and the whites. Poor missionaries did not have much use, not to mention money, for the said hair products and items of the Chiefs interest. What they did have was the white man's Bible, and a lot of it. Soon little Talking Bird could, and was, reciting sermons that could place any traveling preacher on the shame list. They now had a plan of their own. She was returned to camp by the missionaries with a smile of assurance that through her, being one of the tribe, their work would be done in no time flat.

Needless to say, the tribe was not happy in the least about this new development. Her name was changed to "Talking Book". A trade was made as soon as possible when the girl reached young womanhood for something of more value, a load of rifles. The men they traded with were the same ones we left behind in the mountain cabin. These were rough, hard drinking men. The kind of men who didn't care if the guns they traded would kill innocent people. The Chief took a chance, made his bet, and lost his only daughter over men's hair tonic.

5

Life in the West could many times be a lonely and restless place. It made for hard living and hard people who most often died before they reached old age. Even though Talking Book and I were partners on the trail, we sometimes needed a little change of company. There were times when we came upon little towns with shop windows to look in and other people to look at. We always had a kind of unspoken code between us around other folks. We agreed to stay away from notice and look out for trouble. The code kept us in line and from letting on to our secret.

There was a lot going on at that time between Indians and whites. Talking Book was looked upon with sour expressions in most places. She stayed with the horses in a safe spot while I walked about sometimes. One trip to town in particular, was the start of the most fearful time for both of us that I can remember.

*

My old worn boots bumped along the wooden planks of town. Store windows, moving people, horses, turning wheels, and dust when there wasn't mud. I caught a reflection of myself in the glass. I was getting taller. At the same time, there was a young woman about my age that passed by the glass. I made the mistake of comparing the two reflections. She had soft flowing hair under a pale pink hat. Her dress was made of clouds it seemed as she floated above the boards with hardly a sound. I could smell a hint of some flower that reminded me of my mother's room. The men on the boards moved aside, tipped their hats, and then she was gone.

I stared at the glass and at my reflection. I looked down at my rough and cracked hands. A heavy feeling filled my chest. It was then I felt that I had been robbed of something. My childhood? My girlhood? A decent life? The anger I felt was burning me alive. I could hardly breathe from all of the feelings that needed to be stuffed back down. I willed my boots to move that felt like filled water buckets and I ducked into the General Store to escape. It was the bell on the door that brought me back to the present. All eyes were on me, a quiet filled the place. A quick list of supplies filled my mind and raced out of my mouth to the man behind the counter. He began to fill my slim order and business went back to usual.

I was staring at the products on the shelves when the storekeeper figured up my bill, with it came a short string of questions I wasn't ready for.

"Where ya from? What do folks call ya? Are ya passin through? Where ya headed?"

Now you think that I would have had this question list filled for security purposes in situations such as this, but I hadn't. So in a pinch, I blurted out some made up starting place and destination. The in-between I kept fuzzy. It was the name that tripped me up for the rest of my life. My eyes lit upon the first advertisement that could be seen upon the wall behind the man's head. It was a picture of a large round Mexican man, with a large round sombrero, and a bigger than average greased up black mustache. It said, "Cisco Peach Pomade. I use no other!" His revolver was held up in the air with grand gesture to let on that he meant business.

It was at the same time the words came out of my mouth, "Cisco Peach" that a blast of gunshot rattled the window and sent everyone in the store to hugging the floorboards. While the rest were huddled under tables or behind the counter, I crept up to the window to see a gunman race up to the store and bust through the glass. I guessed that he had no time for the door and had a thought to rob the owner of supplies. I didn't have time to think, I just pulled the trigger. As he fell, his eyes followed the bullet's path. It led straight to me. A floorboard thump. Silence. There was a stirring of people that surrounded the scene. The store owner looked sideways at me with a slight nod of thanks.

"Cisco Peach. Why, we carry your pomade. Quite popular with the customers."

*

The commotion that followed was quick in coming. We learned that an attempt had been made to rob the local bank. It was the sight of a U.S. Deputy Marshal crossing the street that sent one gunman crashing through the window in an attempt to escape. Now it was known, that most frontier outlaws don't scare easily. It was also known that this particular U.S. Deputy Marshal was a crack shot. He was a hard-nosed and relentless tracker and always got his man. We heard that one look at the Marshal, and the would-be robbers lit off in different directions. Somewhere in the retreat there was a shotgun blast between the men, one being on the boards at our feet with my bullet in him.

This was a reminder to me that it was time to grab my order and head out. Everyone wanted to know who the shooter was and I suppose that the shop keeper was happy to fill them in. Not knowing where this was headed made me nervous. The fact was that there was still one gunman loose, and I did not feel an urge to speak with the Marshal just then. Talking Book and I headed toward the outlands and away from town.

6

Days were getting longer on the plains which were waking up as if from a long sleep. There was a happy feeling to the air that was more like a celebration. Small animals scurried around our horses hooves, already busy at work in the sunshine. It was the time of year when work for us was easier to find and the heaviness of winter was lifting. It seemed that every ranch we passed was alive with activity. Even in the towns we passed there were people running here and there with the dust of wagons and horses mixed in.

We decided to break from the trail for a spell. I made my way toward a card table in one of the town saloons. I was only in a couple of good hands when some big man came across the room and stuck his fat sausage-like finger in my face. He had a huge head with a small roundish hat that looked like it had been squished on with the help of some grease and a few black smith tools. His shoulders were as big as the door was wide and he had suspenders stretched to the breaking point over his middle section. He looked my way over his long greasy mustache and pig-like jaws and yelled.

"Hey, I know who you are. You're that Cisco Peach fella who shot that gunman east of here. I know it by the Indian partner you travel with. Why, you look not much older than a boy. How you shot Chug Gonzales through the heart from the floor is beyond my thinkin'. And you settin' here so calm when you have the law on your trail and Chug's brother too! Why, I use your hair pomade!"

At this point the whole room was turned my way. It was my turn to throw down my hand, which I did. My move caused the whole table to groan at once as I proceeded to scrape the table of my winnings. I stalled for time and could think of only one thing to say in return.

"What did you say his brother's name was?"

The answer to this one question sucked the air out of the room with such force that Talking Book would later tell me that her hat nearly blew off while at the post with the horses.

Sausage Man said, "You mean to tell me you have never heard of Razorface Gonzales?"

I silently stuffed my winnings into my pouch and kicked my boots through the crowd that parted for me. They all wanted to see a real-live, up-close, almost-dead man walking.

*

I relayed the story of Sausage Man to Talking Book who remained quiet for so long that I figured she hadn't heard me right. Then just as I was about to say, "Hey" she stopped her horse and lifted her chin to the West. Her brown eyes lit up with an amber glow and a stray black glossy hair blew past her forehead.

"I believe the Father would have us head West."

I said, "The Chief gives you silent messages now? We have nowhere to go that way."

She nudged her spotted horse in a westerly direction and I naturally followed.

"I am speaking of the Great Father who has been with us from the beginning. He has a plan for us."

Now just the mention of the word "Father" left a nasty, pasty taste in my mouth that made me want to spit, puke, or both. I decided to leave it there in the dust and we rode off toward the west.

7

We heard stories of gunmen from time to time, mostly stretched out larger than life by time and exaggeration. There were men darkened by death, who traded life and lead for little or nothing. Judging only by the brutality of life on the trail, we figured most stories had some truth mixed in. There were tales told around the fires about the Gold Rush in California, where you used most of the gold dust you broke your back for, just to eat or get a drink.

Dime novels told even taller tales of Billy the Kid and Jesse James. It was somewhere between one or one hundred men they killed depending on who told the story. Pictures of murderous gangs and faces of lone gunmen were hammered up for any passerby who had a little time on their hands. For those with limited pocket change, a lucky shot could change the weight of a person's money pouch or his reputation for life.

There was one name on the plains however that flat out stood for the Devil himself on horse back. That name was Razorface. Not many who had a personal visit with this character ever lived to give an accurate account. So the legend grew. It was said that he was a "killer of killers." So deadly and ruthless that none could ride with him except his brother. And I just unknowingly shaved down that pair to a single.

*

In the days of their youth, the brothers Gonzales were somehow connected with a massacre of an entire population at a Mexican orphanage where they were raised. Nuns, children, and animals; all dead and left for the buzzards in the hot desert sun. Local law men found it hard to pin the rampage on the two young boys. They vanished shortly afterward and it was good riddance as far as the locals figured. Their father was said to be a Mexican bandit but not much was known about the mother except that she was Indian.

One thing was for sure. Death rode gladly with the two like a third gun with a grin. The blazing trail of blood that followed them proved the point. It was said that Razorface got his name from a string of cut X marks that ran from ear to ear across his forehead. No one knows how they got there. No one wanted to find out face-to-face, in a matter of speaking.

*

It was as if a black cloud had decided to join us. I saw those X marks in my dreams. People screaming, blood everywhere, and the buzzards swirling above. There were two sure things. We were heading west and my reputation was getting bigger. Town after town we stopped; my story and my made up name got there before we did. It seemed to me that the cloud was traveling ahead to shout out our arrival. Talking Book was more than likely what most gave me away, but I wouldn't let on that my thoughts were drifting in that direction. It was both of us or no dice as far as I was concerned.

We avoided towns after that as much as we could and rode out on the plains which were brutal travel when there weren't any trails. We were rubbing liniment on the horse's legs all the time due to cuts from rough brush or repairing our leather leggings that got scratched up and nearly ripped clean from us. We were being dragged by the pants into what was easily the hardest time of our life.

On one grey and gloomy day, we came over a hill to see the remains of a buffalo hunt. It was like a funeral with only two attendants. There was carcasses skinned and left scattered behind like broken up prairie trash. The remaining meat left to rot. Settlers traveling west just threw things to the side of the trail when their use was up or their wagons couldn't carry the load. They even buried dead loved ones on the trail itself to avoid animals digging them up.

We often made use of things found along the trail, but this time there was nothing left we could use. I was so shocked and sickened by the scene before us that I failed to notice the face of my travelin' partner who had a bigger stake in the waste than I did. It was a passing of an era for her. Her people were born into free roaming spaces. The massive herds of buffalo that thundered through the plains provided life for them.

With her head held high and her eyes looking straight ahead, I could see a great tear that had cut its way through the dust on her cheek. It was like a river cutting its way through the red hills. We didn't talk for a long time after. My mind quickly got back to the trail we were on. If we didn't find a place to hide out soon, we would end up skinned and left to rot like so many of those wasted buffalo. I looked toward the sky to see a black cloud of buzzards swirling overhead.

8

Crack! I heard it hit the tree above me. Our horses spooked and The Red brought up his front in a great heave, almost throwing me off the back end. It was most likely a rifle shot because the shooter was not anywhere in sight. We both had the same instinct, to run and stay alive! We were out in the open and had no idea who was shooting. All I could hear was the wind passing by my ears, hoping all the while that Talking Book was trailing behind me. No more shots.

I don't know how much time passed before we came to a valley. On the far end stood one of the strangest houses I ever saw. As we rode closer we began to see movement. On the front porch of a very tall house that looked more like a box with smoke trailing out of the top, sat a surprised bunch of women in all kinds of wild dress. Now Book and I were women of the world, kinda, we had heard of sporting houses and that was one reason we were puttin' on the hats.

What stood out most to us were the crazy pinkish stripes that traveled around the window frames, not to mention the bear-sized Chinamen who sat next to the door. We had no recourse but to proceed considering our present ride from some unknown target practice aimed our way. We must have been marked as some first-timer, smooth-faced boys who just rode in from the ranch. There was a collection of smiles going around the group. The Chinaman stood up and motioned us to a stop. He grabbed the reins of our horses and pointed to the door. We weren't about to argue. At the same time, we were a bit concerned as to the outcome or lack of evidence as to our *manhood*, as it were.

*

I could smell her as she walked toward us. The woman who filled up the doorway only seconds before was about three of me put together. You would think Talking Book had never seen red hair in her life because her eyes were the size of silver dollars.

"Hello boys! You have just met the acquaintance of Colonel Redbird." She boomed.

She was a mountain of a woman starting with a flame of red hair piled on top of a head that went straight into her shoulders. No neck visible from where I stood. Her massive trunk of a chest went straight again into her trousers, due to the fact that she had no curve where her waist should be. She was a tall pile of boulders with a big leather belt on top of a large pair of cavalry trousers. Those same trousers were stuffed into men's cavalry boots. Her arms were the size of my legs, both of them together, and at the end of her right arm, smashed between her round dainty fingers was the fattest smoking cigar I ever saw. The smoke curling up and up around the mountain of fire. One might hear the ringing of a fire wagon bell wherever she traveled, which of course, was over a long distance in a very short period of time.

As she took inventory of us with her small and piggy blue eyes a sort of recognition came over her. A grin took up the corners of her doughy blushed cheeks. Her assessment was followed in short order by a quick nod of her head. "Well, I suppose you two might need shelter. Chop here will take your horses. We'll get you set up with a room, a hot meal, and as payment, you can set me up with a good story. Welcome to the Bird House!"

With that said, the Colonel gave us a wink. We of course, did as instructed. We made our way toward the Bird House in the midst of a cloud of cigar smoke, amused looking women, following a huge red mountain, and wrestling with an ever-growing concern that we had just been found out and had no choice but to provide as payment, "a good story."

9

He studied the house with his yellowing eyes. The shelter of trees was just enough cover. Waiting was not a problem. Hunting had always been his favorite game. The best hunting game of all started at the mission. The nuns with their rules, their God, and their sticks that they hit you with. What are they hitting at now? They are hitting at the buzzards circling the sun. Around and around and around. Now Chug was gone too. Waiting would not be a problem. He had just begun this new hunting game. It gave him time to plan. Lots of time. He reached up to run a finger along the X marks on his forehead. One for each time he killed someone like his mother. With swift motions he lifted his stained hat, raked his hand through his thick greasy hair, returned the hat, and tried to rub off the memories from his palms onto his pant legs. Over, over, over. The material had red stains from grinding his flesh into them. They reminded him of his past and present, stained red.

He made camp in the dark. It swallowed him up whole but he was comfortable there. There were things in the dark that kept him company. Dark shadows that danced against the sky and wormed their way in and out of his brain, leaving spaces that weren't filled with anything except hate. They helped him to rub the stains into his pants, pushing him on without mercy, grinding the life out of his eyes. Life without Chug hadn't been too lonely. He had plenty of company. He looked out of the dark toward the tall house. One by one, the oil lamps within the house flickered on.

*

Clean skin was a luxury seldom experienced on the trail and in the West in general. I could probably count on both hands the total of the times water had hit my entire skin all at once, crossing a river included. I couldn't count one time where an actual bath tub was involved. I could pare it all down to one finger compared to the experience of the Bird House claw-footed double tub. But let me back up a space.

I was trying to figure how we were stuck into this spot of trouble. Why only one shot? Was someone spookin' us into a trap? We were led through a parlor that looked like a mail order catalog had a red velvet sale and everyone in the house made at least a dozen orders. Walls were covered with fine red woods and polished shiny so that it looked as if ghosts were following the company of the room. The mix of smells of musky wood and cigar tobacco swirled around my head, making me feel sorta dizzy.

There were pictures everywhere of half naked women and birds of every kind. There was one large golden cage with what looked like a hundred yellow birds making the most beautiful sounds, like so many tiny musical instruments. My eyes were drawn to the top of the curving staircase to see a golden twisted pole hanging from the ceiling by two large red velvet ropes. It was as if a large bird was some where in the room and would soon land on the perch at any time. Both Talking Book and I snapped nervous glances about wondering when the unseen fowl would swoop down from the shadows.

The Colonel must have read our minds and she let out a whooping laugh. It was right about this time that my nose caught drift of the most wonderful smell I had ever had up to that point and probably ever will again. It floated from the kitchen, through the house, and grabbed my stomach, which reacted with an ache as if it had never been fed in all its life. I tried to linger but we were being pressed on up the staircase to a row of doors and a large cabinet where we stopped. Swinging open the creaking doors and shuffling around inside, the Colonel appeared with short stack of clothing and two bath towels. We were each awarded with an armful and led to a door with the promise of the clean return of our old clothes.

Behind the door it stood. Large metal claws for legs and big enough for two people. I had never before in my life saw a real bathing tub of white porcelain. My mother used a metal washing tub that we stood up in and froze in the process, so there was no time to take time really. This room had a small bench to the side with a wall rack for hanging clothes you took off. There was a metal rack across the top of the tub for a scrubbing brush and real bar of soap. I was staring and wondering where we would get enough water, when my question was answered by a thump on the stairs.

Two long-faced girls with steaming buckets of hot and cold water appeared. They were wearing short-type boy pants with long sleeve shirts. The two faces looked just alike, with the same crop of brown dots across the nose and over the cheeks like so many seeds spread down on the soil at planting time. Their long reddish hair was braided at the sides and hung down the back. I was so tranced that I hadn't even noticed that the Colonel slipped out. We watched the girls pour and mix the water and then swirl a metal basket with a long handle through also. There must have been soap pieces in the basket because the water appeared soapy right after. The girls stepped out without so much as a look up. The door closed and we stood with our arm loads in silence.

"You first." Talking Book's only reply sounded like a gun shot in my ear.

10

Here we sat in the kitchen at a long wooden table on soft red flowered cushion chairs. We were freshly scrubbed up and given new trousers and shirts just our size with our old ones hanging freshly on the line. Our hair was slicked back tight with fresh pomade. "Chop" the front porch Chinese bear was at the pot on the stove, having made us some sort of cut greens with the most fragrant smelling oils and spices.

"I call him Chop for his unmatched culinary talents." The Colonel informed us. "His true name is Lee and he is the only love I have ever known. The fact that he is my size gives him all the edge he needs. We met in San Francisco on the docks, or should I say under."

At this comment, she gave a sideways grin toward the Chinese mountain and he gave a quick nod of his boulder shaped head. He served up plates for us and we shoveled in the contents of what I can only describe as heaven on earth. There were spiced chunks of meat and vegetables with a wonderful liquid swirling around it. The Colonel continued her tale.

"I was running a small house with a few girls and doing pretty well for myself in San Francisco. I happened to make enemies of a local officer of the law, which was my downfall. I found one of my girls nearly beaten to death. She was able to spit out her attacker's name through a pair of bloody lips and died shortly after. I figured I would "do the right thing" and report what I had heard to the police chief through a business associate of mine. You see, many officials were customers also. Two men paid me a visit one night. I ended up half dead and tied to the bottom of one of the docks waiting for high tide to roll in. Chop here found me, hauled me in like a soggy old fish, and took care of me till I mended up. He never asked who I was or where I'd been. After that, we headed inland. We made our way cooking for miners and various other enterprises. I eventually bought this land and built me this house where you're sittin' in the kitchen. Now it's your turn."

*

He moved with the shadows from one tree to the next. Invisible in the darkness that was his constant companion. Night creatures cowered and scattered before his presence, as if they could hear the twisted mechanism of his thoughts, turning and turning. Along the side of the barn the shadow passed to the back of the house where the kitchen lamp burned. The light made a quick halt within inches of him, not wanting to come within the slightest inch of his features. It reflected off of his eyes. Eyes that were searching back and forth like a night-stalking predator. His shot at the two had done just what he wanted. They were spooked into a hiding place. Trapped in a cage. He was rubbing his stained pants again. Over and over.

*

I eventually opened my mouth to speak when Talking Book held up a hand. "The birds." She held her finger to her mouth after she spoke.

That quick, all ears were tuned toward the cage in the parlor. She was right; the birds had quit their music all together. It was at that moment that out of the corner of my eye I caught it. A shadow figure like an arm reached for me. Behind and through the curtain it came, reaching and clawing like a lifeless, dead tree branch. It floated through the curtain without a sound. I froze and felt the thick blackness of death choking off my breath and beating my heart all around my ears.

Talking Book turned my way with widening eyes and looked past me toward the window where the shadow reached. She stood up almost knocking over her chair and reached out her palm in the same direction, murmuring something under her breath. The Colonel was up and at the window in two steps, yanking the curtain back. She had not seen what we saw. She could only look at us with a puzzled stare.

"This window is locked up and lily pale is a mighty certain description of what you look like. It's black as ink out there so if you claim to have seen something I would sure like a hint of what the devil it could be."

"You have spoken the last part correctly" whispered Talking Book.

Talking Book's assessment dropped the temperature in the room, killed the mood for conversation, and moved the three of us into leaning toward the only heat source and the biggest presence in the room. The Chinese bear gave a quick look at Talking Book and an equally quick nod of his boulder head as if in agreement. We sat in an uneasy silence and watched the steam curl up from the pot Chop was stirring. The food lyin' like a rock in the bottom of my gut.

The sound of hooves and a wagon followed by a rap on the door tore our attention away from our quiet moment. If it weren't for the pounding of feet on the floor above us, I probably would have forgotten all about the other people in the place. I was so caught up in my own nightmares that the sound of The Colonel's voice gave me a jump where I sat.

"Well! Put on a smile *boys*, it's time for business at the Bird House! I'll be getting that story from ya later on Cisco. Of course you're welcome to come into the parlor for the show." She winked when she said it and then disappeared into the parlor where the birds had started up again. I couldn't remember ever giving her my name.

11

Spying from the shadows, just outside the light, he watched them at the table. He was reaching in with his eyes, into their thoughts and fears, searching for weakness that he could trap and save for later use. The Indian was harder to figure. He couldn't reach that one the way he could the other. He could taste fear. It sunk into his skin and caused his heart to pound with vengeance. The one with the pale skin was growing paler by the second. He wished to reach in right then and rip that pale throat out with his fingers.

The blackness was pushing him on like all the times before, dancing across the sliver of a moon and around his head. He rubbed his stained pants in anticipation. A second later it was all shattered by the Indian. She had jumped to her feet and reached toward him. The dancing had turned to shrieking screams piercing through his brain. He clamped his hands over his ears and took a few steps backward. Something was coming. The sounds of horse's hooves were pounding toward the house.

*

Talking Book and I stepped with caution down the dark hall toward the growing light of the parlor. The place had filled with customers. There was loud laughter and a happy tune playing on the piano by one of the girls in an outfit that I can only describe as bird-like. Green tail feathers shot up her back and swayed like prairie grass as she played. She wore a sparkling green dress that hugged her waist and continued up to her chest that was spilling out over the top. I kept my eyes peeled to the top of her head where her reddish gold hair was pulled up into a curly mass with feathers sticking out of the very top. Like a green sparkling bird.

She laughed a sweet musical laugh as she played but when she turned toward us; it was her eyes that caught my attention. They had a sad and lonesome look. As if she had too many nights of playing piano and pretending to laugh. Like a caged bird that looked out over freedom beyond the bars and dreamed of soaring over the treetops with the warm wind racing past her feathers.

I looked around to see if anyone else noticed this, but none seemed to. I looked toward my companion who had her face turned upward and was staring with steel eyes toward the top of the stairs. What swooped down upon us was a bird of a different kind.

She gripped the side of the giant perch that swung from the ceiling. She had a glare that reminded me of a giant hawk who had just spotted a fat prairie dog too far from a hole. The music changed into a louder and angrier pounding of the keys and all eyes were on the perch. Her outfit was blood red with stockings to match. She was covered in red jewels that seemed to match perfectly with the color of her blood red lips and coffee colored skin.

She had dark hair, almost black that hung about in a wild fashion with feathers floating from her waist like a skirt.

I heard a loud clang from behind me and turned to see that Chop had hit a large round metal object of some kind with a large wood hammer. I figured this was a signal of some kind because the bird of prey swung down on the perch over our heads with a whoosh of perfume and swirling feathers. Back and forth she swung. She was the most beautiful grown women I ever seen.

That's when the rest of um came down. All colors you could think of; blue, yellow, orange, purple. Like a sunset. The colors ran into each other and you couldn't pick out one you liked best. Laughing and sparkling all the way down the stairs. The customers just clapped their hands and couldn't wait to snap one up into their arms. All the while the piano was playing with the birds singing along.

*

He weighed his options. Time to wait and watch. He began making special plans for the Indian. He had a history with his mother's people. He hated her for leaving him and his brother at the mission. He left his mark on many like her, leaving them hanging with outstretched arms and legs in the shape of an X, the same X carved on their foreheads. One on his head for every one he killed, counting only the women. The X marked the spot where his soul had once been.

Maybe this one's hand would look nice dangling from his saddle. The same one that reached toward him in the kitchen. It would hang, dried and shriveled and dead like his brother was. He turned then and disappeared into the night but he was not alone. The shadows ran blindly ahead of him. Racing to escape that same out-stretched hand of Talking Book.

*

I don't want to get into a long conversation about the workings of your average western sporting house. There's plenty of tales you could read yourself if you were of a mind to root um out. One thing's for sure. The faces I have seen have had painted on them a long, hard road of selling minutes of their life off bit by bit. One day you have sold off so many parts that what's left is only a shell of skin and an empty set of eyes that are longing for something long ago lost. I watched them pair up after a while and head up the staircase. They had alcohol-false smiles and painted faces with empty eyes.

We stood by while the Piano Bird ran her hands across the keys for the last time. She barely brushed her hands on the last few keys. The sound it made was like the distant whimper of a small, lost child, longing to be held safe by a loved one. Even the birds were singing in their own sad way. It touched my soul and I reached out to touch her silk-spun crown of reddish hair. She turned her empty eyes toward us and the corners of her mouth turned up ever so slightly at my kind gesture.

The two red-headed children showed up from out of nowhere and huddled next to the piano player while she played them a little tune. I thought I saw a hint of happiness in them but it was hard to tell for sure.

"Well boys! How bout we retire to the porch for a smoke and conversation?" Colonel Redbird had burst upon the scene with her usual flare for grand entrance.

12

We sat on the wooden porch. A carpet of stars twinkling above us. The Colonel was sitting in a dark corner. The glowing ember of her cigar looked like a steam train pushing through the night on lonely tracks. I could see Chop sitting in a tall-backed chair inside reading a fancy covered book under the lamplight. Talking Book was sitting silent but alert. We couldn't escape the shadowy presence that made its way into the kitchen earlier. It was reaching out for us from the darkness that surrounded the house.

I took a deep jagged breath and for better or worse, tried to tell the story of my life up until the present. The two behind me just listened. There was a feeling in the cool night air of a kinship between three trail-weary travelers. In our own way we had each fought through life the best we could with what we had. I felt older than my years by now. My bones had an ache too deep to put into words. I was glad for the dark and the silence of my companions. Then it came. A slow moving warm trickle down my scrubbed cheek. It shocked me at first and I wiped at it fiercely with the back of my hand.

At length, the Colonel spoke. "Some of us fight against our gender and turn into men out of necessity. Others of us keep our womanhood and fight to live life on our own terms. We shove away the cold stares and harsh words. All the while pretendin' that we don't live in a man's world to begin with. We know from experience that we have little say to speak of. For the most part, I've always felt like this business for me was a nasty one.

"Why, most times it's the same law abiding kinds that don't think twice about dragging us through town on the back of a wagon to the local jail as a fine example of how they are 'cleaning up the place.' Those same *citizens* show up on my porch to be first in line come Friday night. They build their schools and line their pockets with the money they skim from us and from our trade. I could sit out here all night long with tales of heartache that would make your stomach turn.

"Take the two red-headed young twins we got in there. Chop and I passed by their shack in our travels, only to almost be knocked off our wagon by the stench of death that came from it. Their mother had been dead for days. Their drunken pa hadn't felt the need to take the body out and bury it proper. He was ready to sell the two to the first whore trader that could come up with a fresh bottle for him. I told Chop to throw him a bottle and took the two six year-olds in, all the while promising myself never to put them to work in the trade. I offer them the best I can here but it doesn't take the death from their eyes.

"I can see it in the girls too but you know they have it better here than most places where they'd get sick, beaten, robbed, or worse. We keep them healthy and alive. For most of them, this is the only family life they've ever had. It's the first time they feel like they belong somewhere. You know, it's been said that our kind have no friends on the outside of our world and ain't no flood of pity is gonna rush into the souls of the good people for our benefit. I'll be hanged if there ain't laws in place that will protect the common dog from abuse but not a one to protect women of vice! "

It was Talking Book who broke her silent vigil and did so with her usual flare for hope glimmering and vision that could have only come from a source that I was yet to stumble upon. "Where there are no oxen, the manger is empty, but from the strength of an ox, there comes an abundant harvest."

Now, I was just about sure we were going to be kicked into the night and on our way after that comment but to my surprise, the Colonel piped in with gusto. "And where there ain't no bull, there ain't no crap and when there ain't no crap, there ain't no garden, and boys, we got enough crap between us to stretch a green belt across the Great Plains for sure! Maybe we've been going at this thing all wrong. Why, I bet if we can put our three heads together, we can come up with a profitable enterprise that doesn't make us a constant bunch of the walking dead. "

Silence filled the porch once again as we tried to imagine life differently than the way we've lived it so far. I spoke my mind, which tended to be of the glass half-empty kind. "What in Pike's name have the three of us in common? Book and I on the trail and me with the cards trying to make bread out of dust. I've had trouble with a happy trigger finger too. No offense Colonel, but you

45

with your sporting deals ain't gonna cut it with us. We took to our ways to get away from that life and what it brings."

Book's turn. "We know riding. She knows money."

The Colonel cocked her head and stood up with a heave, shoving her chair back. "Boys! I think I've got it! Let me converse with Chop in private. We'll all meet in the parlor come sun- up."

*

On the ridge above the house perched two riders with the gentle puffing of their horses breathing behind them. They couldn't afford the light of a fire. They were trailing a killer and this particular U.S. Deputy Marshal had never lost a man yet.

13

Sun up started with a loud gong from a large wooden hammer. We were the last to trail down the steps and were met with a groggy group of ruffled feathers, wondering what the fuss was all about.

The Colonel spoke to the group. "We are called to a time of decision here at the Bird House. I have a proposition for anyone willing to stay on with us." There were confused looks all around as the group tried to sort out the meaning of '*stay on with us.*'

She started speaking again, "I spent the night with the contents of my life rattling around in my head and hit on the idea that all my gain has been for ill. I have accumulated not much more than a handful of heartache and a long list of regrets. It's no coincidence that most women of the sporting profession we are in end up in a wood box. You can visit them on the outskirts of the town cemetery with nary a marker.

"I would like to propose the idea that a new beginning can be had with some hard work. And the work starts here, with whoever is willing. The rest can go as they please with enough pocket change to start with and a ride to town. From here on out, the house and land will be called the Flying Bird Ranch. My idea is to raise and breed horses that we can sell to people in need. Any of you with a mind for change and talents to offer in this area, will be asked to stay on and will be given a share of the profits.

"Ladies, it's hard times that break the weak but make the strong even stronger. We have had enough hard times to knock a crowd of men flat dead. There ain't a one who can tell us we can't run a ranch! I'll need to know your answer by noon. At that time Chop will make a run into town with those who choose to move on."

*

There haven't been more than a couple cross conversations between me and Book. As we sat in our room after the Colonel's speech, I made a long list of reasons why I wasn't ready to stay on at the "ranch." I threw out the fact that I was being chased by who knows what out on the trail. It was looking pretty good to me to keep riding and take my chances. It had been my way of things for a while now and I wasn't sure I wanted to give it up. I wasn't even carrying my own name! No one seemed to care about the fact that the man on the poster looked nothing like myself, who by the way, could never sport a large black mustache! What did I care about helping out a group of tired working girls and that red mountain of a woman that I barely knew? If I stopped now, my past could come crashing behind me and I would have to deal with it. All my feelings were crammed down and waiting to leak out for all to see. Book stayed silent and listened to my ranting.

"And don't you look at me with those eyes of yours! I've had it up to here with your words of hope and wisdom! I have an idea to get shut of this place! Just what can we do here? Haven't I done too much already with my trigger fingers and my big mouth? Which one of those useless feathered girls do you want to drag up on a horse and teach to ride? Who'll buy from a retired bunch of whores and a couple of hat wearin' girls? Haven't we got enough of our own trouble already?!"

Talking Book looked up at me with a fierce stare. In her eyes I could see a war party that had already set fire to the wagons and was riding in the wild circle of victory. They blazed with a wicked kind of light. She addressed me in a low growl that I'm sure she saved especially for her worst of enemies.

She clenched her teeth and growled, "I watched you kick in a shack door and stand up to two of the worst kind of men to save a lost Indian girl. I see no difference between myself and this house of lost souls."

*

The morning light broke through the trees. The shadows of the branches making jagged lines across his face. He closed his eyes again, not wanting to come face to face with the light so soon. The buzzards were swirling in his dreams. Screams and smoke and the sound of guns. Dreams of death ran through his head. Even these were better than facing the light. He pulled his hat down over the X marks on his forehead.

*

I hadn't noticed that Chop had left the kitchen. I was so deep in thought during the meal. I heard the wagon being pulled round and the front door swing open. Book and I had been eating in silence and hardly looking at each other. Around my head a whole flock of what-ifs were on the wing. I jumped when I heard the stomping of feet from the stairs and the bumping of what was probably a trunk or two being dragged on down to the parlor area. We took a quick glance at each other and headed in to see what was next to come.

14

Wilson "Boots" had been a Civil War informant working under Allan Pinkerton. As a U.S. Deputy Marshal he trailed all kinds of criminals and had been involved in all kinds of assignments. He worked at it harder than most. Being a black lawman was not an easy job, even out West. There was still the slavery of thought that said the color of your skin made a person "less than." The simple fact that he was still above ground spoke louder than words. He couldn't shake the idea that this case stank to high Heaven. He could smell it and don't ask him how.

Tracking criminals and lowlifes was his game. He and his partner Abel had been trailing a string of bloody bodies across the plains. Bodies that were tied up and left in the shape of an X. No regard for man or women that he could tell. The women are what got him. His own mother had been murdered in cold blood, which is why he chased these killers with such ruthless determination. Who could've done the things that he saw? Only the faceless monster hiding somewhere in the trees, probably watching him now through the darkness.

The killer was always one jump ahead of the prints he left behind in the dirt. Boots couldn't figure if he had a partner or maybe a lookout man. That idea came crashing to a dead-end every time they saw the single tracks leading away from the scene of each bloody crime. The only thing Boots could do was to bury the remains and keep riding, hoping to catch up. Never mind the fact that Indians didn't like being buried in the ground. He could only do what he could and let the Almighty sort um out.

A young gunman shot and killed his brother Chug in town. That was one down. The other, Razorface Gonzales, had been a wanted figure in every lawman's book. He was wanted and blamed for many murders that came along, especially if they were unsolved. The only thing that was missing was the face. No one *alive* could describe him. All wanted posters were marked with a large X and a short description of name and crimes committed. The bounty on his head changed as often as the tales associated with him. Boots had long ago decided that he would follow him to Hell if that's what it took. He was willing to gamble that Hell's border was up ahead at the end of a trail that led to two young riders. They were holed up in a sporting house in a little valley right below where he would be waiting.

*

From where we stood it seemed divided pretty even. There were girls who stood at the door with traveling bags in hand and tears in their eyes. On the other side stood three who were in what I could only think were left behind pants and shirts from past customers. In the pants stood a stocky-framed blond, the piano bird, and to my shock and amazement, behind the others, stood the dark haired bird of prey.

In came the Colonel with envelopes in her hand for each departing girl as promised. It was known all around that a person's word was as good as a written contract, even if that person was a sport house-owning madam. The wagon was loaded up for town and sent off as planned. The ones left behind stood waiting for orders while Book and I stared each other down, waiting for the first one to draw a breath. It was the moment of great decision. I thought about what would have happened if I had left right then. The trail was practically pulling at my neck like a hemp rope at a public hanging. Would she have left or stayed? I'll never know because something was keeping me in that spot and stuck to the floor and that's where I stayed.

It's a mystery to me that a person always feels more comfortable doing the same thing over and over expecting something different to happen. For once in our lives, we had to do something we had never done to gain something we had never had. I had been running a long time and was afraid to stop. There was a cold, deep fear of the unknown. True freedom required death as payment. Death of my old ways of surviving and thinking was a painful thing. It would be something I would struggle with for the rest of my life.

"Well then! I thank the rest of you for stayin' on with us. Let's head to the table and see what we have to work with."

The Colonel had spoken and we all trailed in behind her to the kitchen table to take an inventory of the situation. Just about the time she drew in a breath there was a noise from the hallway. We looked in the general direction to find the two red heads peek around the corner with wide eyes. The Colonel smiled.

"Don't you fret little ones. I won't be shipping you off anytime soon." They looked at each other and without a word, reached out their arms and hugged tight. My throat tightened up, which I hated of course.

The Colonel continued. "First off let's all get acquainted for the benefit of our new partners. Keys, we'll start with you."

At this, the piano bird spoke up in a melodic sing-song voice. "Lillian Keys. The name came before the piano." She shot a grin around the group. "I was raised on a Southern plantation and my daddy bred prized horses. He beat his horses and his women. I can ride any man into the ground. It ain't gonna be side-saddle neither!"

The stocky blond let out a whoop and took her turn. "Della's the name. But then I've gone by many others, Goldie, or Doll usually. My momma was a sportin' woman. God knows who my pa is. I definitely ain't a fair beauty, but I'm strong. I've been in the game all my life and seen enough to tell ya that I don't want to die like my momma. She was poisoned with a quack doc's mercury treatment. I can shoot and ride with the best and I sure as hell ain't goin down without a fight."

All eyes went to the next speaker who sat staring straight ahead. A deep, rich voice filled the room and held the rest at the table in rapt attention. "I am Lupé."

The Colonel piped up again. "Now ladies. I would like to introduce to you Talking Book, sitting next to *her* is the infamous Cisco Peach."

This statement from the Colonel sent a look of recognition and wide eyes between two of the girls. A small grin started to spread over the face of the dark one for the first time I'd ever seen.

15

Out on the plains, the small band of warriors stopped. Two riders jumped down silently and searched the area of the murder. There was no body left but there was a clear trail of hoof prints and cut ropes lying in the dust where the victim was tied to X-shaped crossed logs. One of the men bent down, came back up with a red bead pinched between his fingers, and held it up to the sun. The surface of the bead reflected a fierce look in his eyes. They burned bright like the blazing sun above. He then scanned the area for any sign of recent digging. His gaze landed on a mound of dirt which would be their next destination. It held the body of a loved one of the tribe. It wasn't the first time they came across a scene like this.

*

After introductions, the Colonel produced a paper from one of her pockets and lit her cigar. We waited silently as the smoke began to mingle with the morning light gliding through the window. It wound around the page she was holding up.

"One of the customers had this on his person and I had one of the ladies "borrow" it for our benefit." She read out loud for us an advertisement for a stock sale to the west of where we were.

> **GREAT WESTERN STOCK SALE**
> **COME SEE THE BEST STOCK IN THE WEST!**
> **ALL BUYERS WELCOME -**
> **FINE RIDING AND RANCH STOCK AVAILABLE**

When she was done the Colonel looked around the group and laid out her plan for our approval. "I heard a customer flapping his jaw about this stock sale and showing this advertisement around last night. I remember thinking I could turn a profit for myself if I could only run this place like a ranch and get out of the other business altogether. I thought the idea was just a whim until I talked with these two on the porch."

All eyes and attention were turned toward Book and I. The Colonel spoke again. "In my line of work, I'm a business woman first. I have many contacts that will be valuable to us, including military officers who are in constant need of horses. Its horses that make more sense to me. They are smarter and easier to herd. I figure that if we start with some good animals, we can have the best herd for miles around. My family owned a large ranch before I joined the sisterhood. I chose to change my name like most to keep my family from shame. My plan is to take back that shame one horse at a time.

"The next few months we'll gather up all we can sell from the house, buy supplies, and get this place fitted for ranch work. I have a few people in the sporting business who would like some of our finery. We can paint the pink stripes and put in some more practical in-house items. We are better off than most. We have a good house and barn to start, and we are in a natural valley that protects us from harsh weather. We will need to use Chop for some of the heavy work and we'll all have to put in some fencing.

"When we're ready we'll send a few of you off to the sale. You that go need to bring us back the best string of breeding mares you can buy with our money. You can definitely plan on bringing your guns. There are other parties in these hills who make a bad habit of taking what does not belong to them to turn a profit."

At this, one of the "hands" at the table mentioned, "Where are we getting our stallion?"

The Colonel looked out toward the barn where The Red was being kept, then turned to look at me with a grin. "Now Cisco that is one fine animal you rode in on. I'm not one to pry about another's possessions, but if I'm right, that horse is southern bred, top quality, and can run for miles without even breaking a sweat. How you came about him is none of my business but with the right mares, we can't loose. What do you say?"

*

Abel knew that Boots took his time in cases such as this and was real careful in pressing the matter. They had been on the ridge above the house for a little over a day to keep watch. Not much talk passed between the two comrades. They had been riding together for a long time and knew each other too well for there to be much talk. Both lived long past the decision about wives and family. They chose to ride with each other as companions instead. Whenever some wise crack came along about him riding with Boots he would just say, "I'd rather ride on this side of his gun than out in front." No one argued that point.

Still, Abel felt restless. Maybe it was the string of messes they had been cleaning up. It was almost more than a man could bear. And Boots could take a lot. There was an unseen presence in the air. A sickening cloud they were following that threatened to suck the breath from a man's throat. He finally spoke up.

"Don't you feel...?" He was cut short.

"We can't go in now. Hang tight old friend. Yep, I feel it too. Remember we are lawmen first. Stick to the things we can *see*."

16

Let's just say that I didn't say anything for a few minutes. The Colonel shot a glance in the direction of Book who looked her in the eye and answered. "My people are born on horseback. We use the older ones for women, old people, and children to do everyday chores. We would trade many things for the red horse. He would belong to one of our great warriors or even the Chief. I think that he would also have many great children."

All eyes turned back in my direction and I finally spoke up. "My old man never gave a damn about anyone in his life but himself and that horse. He kept houses like yours in business with the money he kept from me and my ma. I find it only fitting that it would be his horse that made the money to shut the old Bird House down and build up the Flying Bird Ranch. And if there is a Hell, then I can only hope that every coin that hits our palms sends an echo down into his forsaken soul. Count me in!"

I stretched my hand toward the Colonel to shake on the deal and did not look in the direction of Book but knew all the time that her golden eyes were dancing with pride in my direction.

"Well partners, we're off and running!" Shouted the Colonel, "We have a load of hard work to do and a short time to do it! Lupé, Keys, and D, I want you to come with me and gather up everything we can sell and take over to Alice's Place. She has the money to burn over at her house since she's doing so well. What she don't want, she'll help us find someone who will. Cisco and Book, you can head outside and give us an idea on what we need to change in the way of fencing and whatnot. From this day out friends, were in the horse business!"

*

Day stretched into night when the moonlight danced and the creeper came from out of the trees. He moved silently from shadow to shadow as if they were old friends. He noticed that some of women had left during the day but no matter. He had decided that after he had hunted the two, he would return and kill the rest for keeping them.   He was waiting for his chance. Somewhere away from the house where he could be alone with the two. No matter how long it took he would watch and wait. He liked to take his time.

*

Up on the ridge the two men squinted into the darkness.
"I think I saw a shadow move but I can't be sure." Abel whispered, trying to squint one eye instead of two this time.
After a minute Boots whispered back, "I might not be able to see a shadow but I feel one and that's what gets me. In the dark your eyes can sometimes play tricks

61

but I never had my gut play um on me. He's out here alright. There was no one following that rig with the Chinaman and girls earlier which leaves our two boys holding up here for whatever reason. Where they are, he's gonna be until we have another mess to clean up. I just hope the kid's just as fast as his hunter is. That's if we don't get to this monster first."

*

With the sundown came the same uneasiness as the night before. We spent the day sizing up what we were getting into and now the house had settled down for the night. I wish I could have said the same for my nerves. Then Book did something I have never heard her do. Lying there in the dark she began to sing a quiet song in her language. I didn't know the words but soon found myself asleep. There were no horrors hiding for me in my dreams, just a peace that overcame me for the first time in a long time.

17

In the days that followed there was a bustle of activity around the ranch. The girls were inside collecting up anything of no use in daily ranch life and hauling it out to the wagon for Chop to drive into town. We sent him off with high hopes of profit.

The wagon was quick to return with building materials and other supplies. Chop informed us that he passed around word that the Bird House was changing trades. I suppose we had our share of scoffers but it didn't stop us from going ahead with our plan. The work was hard, especially for the girls who weren't used to working outside. We all had blistered hands and sore backs, but by the end of the day we actually felt good about something we'd done. This was a new feeling for all of us.

The time came to have a meeting by the barn to address the question of more horses. We had Book's spotted pony, The Red, and a draft we were using for the wagon and heavy work. This wasn't gonna lean in our favor when we had to travel in a group to the stock sale. We also had to decide who would go and when. We needed to buy two or three ranch horses for the work ahead.

It was decided that Chop would drive two girls into town and bring back a small string of three ranch horses. The two girls would ride and they would pull one horse behind the wagon for the trip home. The Colonel brought out five matchsticks with two cut shorter than the others. We all looked around the group and I noticed that Book was distracted by something she saw in the distance.

I looked in the same direction where she was staring. I thought I saw a horse, but as soon as my eyes could focus, it was gone. She looked straight ahead and clenched her jaw. Even from where I stood, I could see a spark of recognition, then a smolder of anger inside. She looked toward the sky and squeezed her eyes shut, moving her lips only slightly. Just then I remembered the others, who by now, were standing in a stunned silence and looking to me for a translation of my partners strange actions. I shrugged my shoulders and stepped up to take one of the match heads sticking out of The Colonel's clenched fist.

I decided to talk about the rider later in private and get Book's take because her answer might not be as welcome to the rest of the group. The rest took my cue and picked sticks. Book picked last. It would be D and Keys who rode in for the horses. The rest of us would wait and keep working. I looked over to see the slight relief on Book's face. I wondered exactly what she saw in the distance.

*

"A band of four." Boots held his looking glass out in front of him and squeezed one eye closed.

Abel squeezed his one eye along with Boots even though he didn't have a looking glass himself. "I'm thinkin' they might be followin' the string of bodies we been puttin' in the ground. This ain't in our favor though Cap."

Boots had long been past the point of telling his partner that he didn't qualify for "Captain" of anything. He just passed over it and kept looking ahead. "Their brand of justice says that they can avenge the death of a loved one. There are some cases, in particular, this one, where I have to agree with their way over ours. There's part of me that would like to see this animal end up like his victims."

Abel's eyes both opened wide as he looked over at his old partner who just kept staring straight ahead through his looking glass. He was watching a band of warriors vanishing into the hills.

*

The wagon was hitched and the three travelers were ready for the trip to town. We tried to outfit them with enough firepower to protect them on the trip. Let me tell ya that anyone with half a brain packed hardware when traveling on the frontier. Most everyone carried a rifle, one or two pistols, a sharp knife usually tucked in a boot, a canteen of water if you were real sharp, jerk meat of some kind in case you got stuck without game, and maybe some ground up coffee. A lot of folks didn't favor the rifle on horseback because they felt it got in the way but I can say from experience that it's better to be prepared than be out-gunned any day. Chop packed himself the Colonel's own Dragoon pistol which would just about put a cannon hole in most things.

They set off over the hill and we went back to making our barn water-tight against the winter. The Colonel went inside and gave me the reins to take up the job.

Book, Lupé, and me were trying to check for warping in the wood, any rot, or anything else we could fix to keep the wind and cold from whistling through. I told them both that I would start at one end and they could start at the other end and we'd move inward. I walked to my start point when I sensed a presence behind me. The next thing I knew there was a Bowie knife against my neck. A cold fear traveled down my legs and set my jaw. I tried not to let panic take over. I hate knives!

I felt a shove and landed hard against the wall boards which dug splinters into my cheek. I turned myself around and saw Lupé standing over me with a look of death in her eyes. She was waving that knife in my face as she spoke in a low nasty tone. "I will never take orders again. Not from you. Not from no man."

18

I am no knife fighter! I use um for hunting and all sorts of other things but not for killing. They make me sick with all that sticking, mess, and whatnot. I just stayed real quiet and still and watched the back of the barn where Book was creeping up in her silent but deadly Indian way.

"Well now Loop, my idea was that we could all work together here. Now, I have no blame on ya at all for gettin' tired of takin' orders and your way of livin'. That's why we're here. That's what we're tryin' to outrun. Ain't none of us better than you. Not a one. Besides..."

She clenched her teeth and stuck her knife closer to my face. "Beesides what?"

"I was just wonderin' why would you bring a blade to a bullet party?"

I let my eyes drift toward her left temple which was about to become real close friends with Book's six gun. Her eyes strayed toward the general area and she presently dropped her knife hand to her side.

"And if you ever come at me again with one of those killin' sticks, I'll shoot you dead. No more partnership needed." I gave a quick nod of thanks to my one true friend.

Our conversation ended and we went back to work but from then on I kept one eye on Lupé, and the other on her knife.

*

Later that night, as I settled down to bed, I wondered why we hadn't heard from the three who went to town today. They were late for sure and that was not a good sign. I was thinking about the events of the day and about what still needed to be done when a shadow crossed by my window. I jumped out of bed and grabbed for my gun. I thought I heard the sound of laughter, faint and far off and ghost-like. It swept into the shaft of moonlight coming through the window and swirled around my head bringing with it fear and trembling.

"Waaait till I get ahold of yoooou" it whispered in my ear. "What your old man did was nootthing. Juuust you waaait...juuust you......"

I was backing away from the sound, shaking my head from side to side when I bumped into something. I looked down to see a pair of legs in the darkness and inhaled a breath to let out a yell like the Devil himself was after me. A hand shot up and covered my mouth from behind.

"Shhh, Shhhhh. Peace!" Book had her arm around me and tried to bring me back from the shock of what had just happened to me. "I saw it too, I will stay here."

We sat in tense darkness until the shadows passed. Just then I thought to ask her about the rider I saw that day and if she saw it too. I was starting to think I was going crazy.

"They were my people riding past our valley. I'm not sure why they were here, but if they wanted us dead, we wouldn't be talking right now. They are warriors. We will know soon enough."

Now this bit of news did complicate things. Where was that wagon? What in Hades was in my window? How did the voice know about my old man!?

*

A talk with the Colonel in the morning led us to believe that we should go to town after the wagon. We still had no word and if there was trouble, we needed to get them back as quickly as possible. Book and I rode out while Lupé stayed behind at the ranch, to my relief. We didn't want to leave the Colonel alone, although I'd bet The Red on her taking on a whole army of Indians with just her looks to shake um up.

The trail felt a bit grand as we were riding together once again; except that I couldn't escape the feeling we were being watched. The trees shook in the breeze and the hills rolled silently along, but I could feel the weight of unseen eyes all around. We didn't speak of it but I somehow knew Book was feeling it too. When she spoke, I nearly jumped off my saddle.

"There are many things that I learned while living with the missionaries. I learned of the Great Father and His Son and also of His enemies. My people also have their beliefs about dark spirits. I believe that we have been visited by these who are our enemies also and wish to do us harm. We can't fight them alone and need the Father's help. I have been talking to Him and will continue. I can see no other way out, but I do believe that we are traveling on the right road. We have much to do yet."

I thought about what she said for a tick and answered, "It's hard on my end Book. You talk about fathers and whatnot but look at what I had to live with and put up with. Sure, my ma had her ways and her Bible but what good did that do her after all was said and done? I'm no better, with all my shootin' and runnin' around like some kind of outlaw. Why, I'm on the down shaft to the bad place, and fast. Look at the girls and what happened to them and their lives. How do they figure in to all this God business? He sure gave them a bad deal. Still, I saw them things come at me and I can feel um yet now. I sure am mighty glad to have you 'round to take up the slack in the upward fashion, if you know what I mean."

She looked at me sideways and flashed me a little grin, then lifted the tip of her fingers against her hat. Just then, we could see the rooftops of town over the hill up ahead.

19

"Bring them whores 'round again!"

"They sure look mighty different in pants don't they?"

"Haw! That one looks better than you!"

Book and I could see Chop tied up and leaning against a hitching post with blood dripping into his puffy eyes. A wagon was being pulled down Main Street with our two partners D and Keys tied back to back and looking beyond hope. D suddenly looked up with an angry face and glared at one of the laughing men. "Go on, laugh it up! Half of ya'll would be up here with us if they treated our customers the same way..."

Her speech was interrupted by the click of a loading shell in the barrel of my shot gun. I was in no mood for talking. Book had her six gun clenched so hard that her brown knuckles were pale. I could see that she would have let um have it too, which was rare in her case. I took inventory of the small crowd that had gathered around the wagon. I saw that one of the men leading the wagon had the Colonel's Dragoon tucked into his belt. His wicked toothless grin spread over his face. The women faded back when they saw us. I noticed that a large number of the men that were yelling loudest, were sure enough out at The Bird House as customers before we changed 'er up.

Someone jabbed someone in the ribs and I heard the end of a whispered sentence. "...Peach fella."

No one drew on us so far. To tell ya the truth, I think they were just stunned about us happening on the scene all together.

"Some fun ya'll are having at other's expense. I suppose you can all tell me what that man there has done to deserve your kindly treatment. How 'bout we untie him so he can tell us all about it. You have exactly one click of my shotgun trigger to get the job done." I pointed my thumb in the direction of Chop.

I looked over toward Book who hadn't moved a muscle and I continued on, staring straight at the man with the stolen dragoon. "Mister, if yer smart, which I figure is probably a stretch, you'll return that gun, cuz the owner will more than likely burn you down later, just on principal alone."

One word out of his mouth led me to believe just what I was figuring from the start. "You'll be plum lucky ifin I don't pull it on the two of you." This was followed by the same toothless grin.

I spit out at him, barely able to hold my finger from squeezing the trigger. "Well now, I figured right. If you think you can beat the two guns trained on ya, then by God I say, give er a whirl!"

His eyes raced back and forth between us and he finally slumped his shoulders. He walked over toward Chop, who was now sitting, freshly cut loose. He was looking miserable on the boards of the walkway with his head in his hands. Toothless held out the gun at arms length toward him with caution.

"While yer at it, dip your hanky in the water trough and dab his head for the love of Mike! For the rest of ya, get those two out of that wagon before my temper flares even more! Cornelius! Haven't you people got better things to do then to rough around hard working ranch hands?"

At the mention of "ranch hands" I was met with several wide-eyed looks. "You heard me right." I said.

I noticed a man slinking his way out of the crowd and turning to run in the other direction. I finally recognized him as a customer and smiled to myself. "Maybe you can tell um just what I'm talking about mister! You sure would know about what goes on at the old Bird House now wouldn't ya?"

All eyes turned toward the fleeing man. Including his wife, who had just balled her dainty fist. He was caught and had no recourse but to answer. "Shut 'er down and turned 'er into a horse ranching outfit."

Shocked expressions came from some of the group and I might have heard a chuckle or two.

"Laugh it up, but not one of ya can say that this here red horse isn't the best you've seen. There'll be more from him at the Flying Bird Ranch for those who have need. We might even forget this little incident if you're quick enough about bringing round that wagon and horses that belong to these you have harmed quick enough."

"I ain't buying from no Indians, Chinaman, and whores!" Some fool decided to pitch his two bits in the pot. This man happened to be a business owner which was to his mistake in my book.

"Well now that would be to your misfortune, cuz we just might decide that when we make a lot of money, your establishment isn't worth our business."

*

On our way out of town we passed by the jail. I looked just in time to see the sheriff give me a tip of his hat. I guess that two women and a Chinese man weren't worth much of his time which was a common thing in those days. Indians were also included in the bunch that didn't get the same treatment as all human beings deserved. This thought made me laugh at the fact that our whole outfit was made up of the categories I just mentioned. One thing did bother me though. If I was so wanted, then why didn't he haul me in?

I was actually glad to be headed back. We had three good ranch horses and our friends all in one piece so to speak. Chop ended up with only a small head wound and we sure all had a good story for the Colonel, which she was always in the mood for.

20

Two horses rode out from behind the jail after the wagon had left.

"Good thing that sheriff takes kindly to us Cap. I'm thinkin' we're all together on trackin' that Razor killer. What do ya make of that Cisco Peach fella? I would have thought a man who killed like he did before would have knocked down at least one lone man back yonder."

"Seems like a good question Abe. I think that there is more to him than we guess. Back East the store clerk told me the Chug shooting was a clear case of self defense. For now, he is our ticket to catching this killer who we don't have *any* guesses about. You can bet he is somewhere watching those two. We'll be there when he decides to make his move."

*

We rode on in silence, with Chop well enough to drive the wagon. I pulled up next to the big Chinese man and decided to throw a question out at him to see where it would land. "How'd you end up here in the West?"

He looked thoughtful and spoke in perfect English. It took me a Texas second to decide that he was the most educated man I had ever met. "My name is Lee On and my family is from the southern part of China in a small village called Kwangtung. We are medical men by trade.

My father and uncles have vast knowledge of Chinese herbal remedies. We traveled to the Gold Mountain because in our country we are very poor. We were hoping to bring our medicines to the mining towns and make our fortune like so many others. Three of us boarded a ship with many other Chinese and came to the city of San Francisco. What we were not prepared for was the hatred toward all Chinese. People wanted opium, not herbs to get well.

"We made a small living amongst our own people and with the few whites who realized that Chinese medicine was far more superior to the alcohol that was being sold to cure any kind of illness. It was then, while fishing by the sea, that I came upon my Cherry Blossom-the Colonel, and brought her to my uncle and father to be treated. Certain authorities found out where she had been taken. They came for us one night and killed my father and uncle. I escaped with Blossom by hiding in a secret room under the floor. We gathered what we could and traveled the camps. There was nothing more I could do. And so, here I am."

"Well Leon, your tale sure proves that you're in the right outfit. I'm sad to hear about your family, but I'm glad to have you with us. We surely can use a man with your mind and strength, not to mention your medicine skills. I have nothing against the Chinese and have witnessed nothing except your hard work and loyal nature. That to me is better than the lyin', drinkin', dishonest, and murderin' ninety percent of the rest of the population!"

I reached out my hand and he grasped it with his bear paw. As he did, I saw a certain sparkle dancing in his eyes that I hadn't seen before.

We pulled up to the ranch with the Colonel racing out to meet us and inspect her precious Chop over every inch of his round head. Our dinner conversation told the tales of our adventure.

21

Bloody meat tasted good, especially when it was still warm and wiggly. It was a good thing that there were so many stupid critters that could be caught with bare hands. His favorite trick was covering up with dirt and leaves and waiting till one of them would crawl over top. Then they would get their necks cracked and eaten up whole. Maybe this would be a good trick to try on one of the cowboys or the Indian. They always figured on being sneaky. They weren't so sneaky roped up to an X of wood waiting to die.

After he ate, he rubbed his hands along his pants and plotted his next move. Sometimes covering up and waiting was the best way to snap a few necks.

*

Work was nearly finished up on the fences and outbuildings. We had a decent house now. All the velvet was stripped away and supplies bought with the proceeds. Our next move was to plan our trip to the sale. This trip would be all of us except the Colonel and Chop, who had healed up nice with nary a mark on his head where the wound had been.

And so, with our trip figured out, the five of us set off over the hills toward the stock sale. I looked over at Lupé. "Why don't you take point and we will follow."

I think she looked a little surprised by this but went ahead with it anyway. You see, I had two reasons for this. One was to give her a chance to lead and improve her mood. Two was to keep an eye on her from behind.

After a full days ride I could tell that the others were gonna be fine on horseback for the rest of the trip. The soft skin on their legs and behind would be sore but with the things they had been through so far, I figured they could take it.

We were all getting tired and were thinking about a place to set up camp, when we came upon a sign stuck into the ground. Leaning sideways, it read:

Travelers Food & Lodging
Baths & Medical Healing
Royal Treatment

There was a funny looking pointing hand in the direction of a crooked path that lead up the ridge.

A fast vote from those of us, except Book who didn't look too happy, decided that we would take a quick look at what was being offered.

*

Behind the group of five riders was a scramble of different tracks. Even if someone was adept at reading sign, they would have had a puzzled look on their face. There was five riders, a lone rider, two riders behind that, and not too far from the trail, a band of Indian warriors taking their time.

"My question is Cap, are we doin' the followin' or is it the other way around? My nerves are racked up and dern if there ain't a shadow or two dartin' around those rocks up yonder."

"Our job is to keep on the track and try to stay low Abel. We need to keep our eyes on that group of five horses. Just keep yourself ready, for anything."

*

"Welcome, welcome! Well bless my soul. The Duchess will be more than pleased."

The person that bowed before us was dressed in a long black coat that was even longer in the back, like a man who drove a funeral wagon. He had round framed glasses which he lifted off of his face when he talked and a tall black hat teetered on the edge of his oily grey hair. He was as thin as a winter branch, had pasty white skin, and sunken dark circles under his beady black eyes.

Behind him stood what could only be a small man wearing a girl's frilly tattered dress. He had his black hair slicked back with a wicked kind of grimy toothed smile. He proceeded to push along a baby carriage that was in front of him. Most of the group had not seen a baby in a long time. We all sort of stretched our necks to see what would pop out of the mess of dirty blankets that were just sort of tossed inside. To our surprise, an even smaller man in a bonnet popped out and nearly caused us to jump from our skin!

"May I introduce the Duchess Arpeggio!"

The dark man had spoken. There was a rustle of purple fabric and a wave of too much sweet perfume. A beast of a woman appeared in the doorway and waved her arm above her head with a tattered silk hanky. She had a tangle of dark ratty hair piled around her head willy nilly like. Her fat body could barley fit out of the door. The folds of her neck came up like hills around her ears. Her eyes cut deep into her painted round cheeks. When she spoke, her whole face jiggled.

"Greetings my lovelies! We have food, rest and libations. Oh and of course, a bath or two maybe? You have already met the professor. Boneilia my darling, show our guests to their rooms, and let me have baby."

We were led toward a ramshackle group of small buildings and paired off. Book and I were in one of the "rooms" and the other three took the one next door. The girl-boy Boneilia slunk away grinning over his shoulder at us like he had a dark secret. He gave me a creepy feeling that began in my lower back area and crawled up like a spider to the top of my head. We looked around the walls which were pasted with medical journals and medicine mail-order catalogs. There were only two stacks of small beds. They were piled one on top of the other like in a bunkhouse with pegs on the walls for clothes. I could not see a wash stand. Book had a grim look on her face which told me to keep my eyes open for trouble.

We walked over to where the others were staying and found that it was a copy of our own room. Keys was peeling off her pants with a look of sheer pain and discomfort. "Why I think I've sprang a leak! Just look at these legs!"

We all looked in that general direction to find that the insides of her legs were covered in tiny blood spots where her hair had rubbed off in the saddle. I was trying to figure a way that we could maybe bring up the stirrups or put a blanket where she sat. These thoughts kept rattling around my head when I heard her saying something.

"Didn't I hear someone say something about a bathing house?"

22

Darkness was falling fast as we headed toward the "bathing house" to take a look. We all took a big breath. It was the most finery we had ever seen, even better than the Bird house claw tub. There were big, fluffy clean linens, imported bar soap, a large tub, a round shaped mirror on the wall, which in the West surely had to travel from somewhere across the ocean or some other exotic place. It had a painted floor with curling shapes of flowers and birds. Sheer curtains hung down from the ceiling like spider webs. It wove its magic around us and drew us in like flies. All except Book, who at this point was backing up slowly.

Boneilia showed up from out of nowhere with a steaming bucket of water and the same wicked grin. He poured the water in the tub and turned around to motion with his grimy fingers, beckoning us toward the bath.

Keys jumped in front of the group and protested, "The injured go first!"

D pulled her pistol from the holster and replied with a grin, "You're lucky I like ya or we could change that to THE DEAD GO LAST." Little did we know that she was almost right.

Lupé, D, and I headed back toward the rooms to let the "injured" bathe alone while we waited our turn. It was then that I noticed that we were missing Book. I let the others head back while I had a look around and began to trail a strange sound that I picked up. I was rounding a corner of one of the buildings when I nearly had my arm yanked out of the socket. I met a pair of wild eyes that belonged to my missing friend.

"What in the..." A hand was clamped over my mouth and I was pulled along the side of a building toward the sound I was trailing earlier.

*

Boots cocked his head to one side looking down on the small collection of buildings below. "Do you remember hearing of any body missing up in these hills?"

"I reckon there to be a few folks that turn up missin' now and again in most places Cap. I tell you what I can't remember hearin' of is a stage stop or bath house or anything close to that in these parts. This must be a pretty new one right cheer."

Boots rubbed his stubbled chin. "That sign back there, this sounds familiar to me somehow. Let's move around to the front. I need to get a better look at the occupants of that main shack.

*

There was the tall dark figure set against the rising moon shoveling the ground and humming to himself. Book shoved her elbow into my ribs and pointed toward the area of the bath house where a smaller figure in a dress was creeping through a hidden door in the back of the building. A feeling of dread came over me and I knew it was time for us to get shut of that place fast. I motioned to myself and pointed toward the bath house. I pointed to Book and toward the room where our riding partners were. She nodded and disappeared.

*

"Well, well, my, my! We will be having a nice meal for our selves tonight eh *baby*? Nice plump visitors we will have."

An unusually small man in infants clothing shook his head up and down at The Duchess who was merrily setting her dining room table... for four. Her wicked giggle floated through the house.

*

I turned the handle to the bath house as silently as I could only to see a wet trail sliding along the floor away from the tub. I followed it with my eyes as a set of small feet disappeared through a secret panel that was beginning to close. I ran toward the closing panel and shoved my boot in what was left of the opening. I heard a low growling curse and felt a knife go through the end of my boot and into the floor boards. I sat down on my behind and used my other boot to kick the panel as hard as I could. Wood went splintering in all directions. I yanked the knife from my stuck boot and threw it to the side, glad that it didn't get my big toe.

I crawled through the hole and looked around. A large meat knife swung past my face. Again with the knives! The back of the bath house looked like a doctor's office. There was a lamp on the table which glittered off of all kinds of doctors instruments. There were saws, knives, and an untold number of other wicked looking tools of torture. There were bottles of strange potions and jars with what looked like human body parts in them. There were other things that I couldn't quite guess at. I held back the urge to get sick. I drew my weapon on the menacing little fellow in a dress who was waving the big knife like an ace.

"Now, I'm not quick about firing on people smaller than me Boney but keep holding that hack tool and we'll have to go round. I just want my friend."

He just stood there grinning at me and I glanced sideways to see Keys laid out on a low table. She had a slow drip of blood running onto the floor from her forehead. I could feel anger rise up like heat into my cheeks and turned back to see a large knife rising up to be thrown in my general direction. I shot him, dress and all.

*

I had Keys leaned up against my shoulder and sort of dressed. We started to head back toward the bunk rooms. I had no idea if anyone else heard my shot but was darn glad that my friend was breathing and with only a small head wound.

Book was crouched down next to Lupé and D who were tied together. She had a gun in one hand and Lupé's knife in the other. The two who were tied up looked dazed and had rags stuffed into their mouths. Book motioned me to silence with her finger to her lips and pointed toward the wall. I gently laid Keys on the bunk and crept quietly toward the wall which began to creek open with a secret panel like one in the bath house. We both stood out of sight and waited while a tall dark figure began to push its way through. I recognized the little tune he was humming as the same one I was trailing in the dark.

I stuck my foot out by his feet and he came toppling over with a crash. His hat and round glasses flew across the room clattering against the wall. Book slammed her gun down hard against the side of his head. All went quiet except for the sound of D yelling something into her mouth full of rags. Her face was bright red and she looked like she would explode any minute. I reached over and yanked her mouth free.

"Let me have a crack at um! I'll kill um dead! Turn me loose I tell ya!"

We let her cool down and untied them both. She wobbled over and gave him a hard swift kick, which landed with a thud in his ribs. She almost fell over with the effort and then sat down to rub her head. Book and I tied the old crow called The Professor up with the ropes, stuffed the rags into his mouth, and gathered up to ride out. We made sure to wake Keys and Book wrapped her head the best she could. Lupé turned toward the bathing house and told us she would catch up. As we rode out into the night we could see the flames of the bathing house spread to the other buildings. The shrill shrieking of the Duchess floated through the flames and darkness.

"B-but Cap! Them there are wanted murderers. Shouldn't we take um in with us? What about those buried folks in them holes?"

"They won't be much of a threat now Abel. I'll send word back to the local law when we get to a town. It seems The Duchess has returned. I heard she was running an outfit that banded together when they met in a traveling circus. The notorious Professor was run out of more than one town for his "medical practices." Right now we need to keep track of our riders. I don't want to lose them and the killer too. He's bound to show up."

*

Flames reflected in their eyes as they passed the scene. All the while the women lumbered back and forth to the well, not able to put out the flames. Had she seen them, she might have called for help.

*

It was a long and rough ride before we came to overlook the town and Great Western Stock Sale. But all were glad to put the latest events far behind us. We had to keep an eye on Keys who was doing much better. We camped and got the rest of the jerk beef out of our saddle bags. Put that together with some dry biscuits and coffee that Chop packed up and it tasted like a regular feast. It was good to get some food in our bellies and rest a bit.

Noise coming from the town drifted up to us sounding loud and strange after we had been in the hills for a couple of days. I still couldn't shake the feeling that we were being trailed. I would have bet my best hand of cards on it.

There was a collection of travelers of all kinds camping round about the town. Through the muddy, smelly streets of town walked and rode hardened cowboys, fancy dressed men, women, children, and everything in between. We rode through and caught a couple of glances. People were running here and there, and we soon melted into the crowd. I figured that this was probably the largest event in this town's history. We talked the night before about our plan to scout out the best stock horses we could find at the best price. What we didn't figure on was that great big sign that jumped up in front of us. It read:

> Ride Dust Devil!
> Biggest, Meenest Bull in the Westurn States!
> Cash Fer Any Who Kud Ride Um!

We all just sat there staring up at the sign when we heard uproar behind us. There was a big crowd of onlookers sitting up on the corral boards shouting, clapping, and making a general ruckus. We all sat up in our saddles to catch a look at the largest, meanest dust cloud we ever saw.

A hapless man gripped a rope with both hands that was tied around the middle of the beast. His eyes were as large as plates as if he were looking death in the face. He was flung off the bull high and wide into the air. He cleared the corral, taking with him a few of the onlookers. The Dust Devil threw himself around like a locomotive, daring the next victim to come forward.

Spit flew in every direction and came down on the crowd like slimy raindrops. I looked over at our group to catch Book's expression but she was gone. I got an elbow in my arm from D, whose face was turning pale as she pointed me in the right direction. Cattlemen with ropes were backing the great beast into a smaller chute for the next rider. Book climbed on the fence to take the next turn. I pushed my way through the crowd just in time to hear a man yell something.

"Hey! No damn Indians."

Another yelled, "The sign says *any* can ride!"

The two men who looked to be running the show shrugged their shoulders as Book climbed on.

*

The local sheriff's office was a bustle of activity. Boots and Abel stood off to the side and waited for a chance to have a few words with the local law. There were two deputies running here and there with jingling keys and shuffling boots. Shouts could be heard from the drunken prisoners in the cells behind the wall of the sheriff's desk. It seemed like something was about to bust from the seams any minute. The town sheriff pinched his red forehead with his stubby fingers. He read the wanted poster on his desk that one of the deputies had pulled from the wall. It had a big X posted on the front. He jumped up at one point, whipped around from behind his desk and slammed the wall with his fist several times.

"Shut up in there or I swear I'll hang ya myself just for lack of cell space!"

Of course this did nothing to quiet the noise and he plopped back down in his chair and began pinching his head tighter. "I'll thank ya kindly Boots to keep an eye on the matter. You can see that I got a pocket full of hornets' bout now."

There was a crash behind the wall and another round of shouting.

"The sheriff jumped and shouted, "For the love of.... gotta go Boots! Keep me posted!" He disappeared behind the door with a slam.

The two made their way down the board walkway through town. They were heading toward the roar of a small crowd where the stockyard was.

24

You didn't have to be too smart to know that The Dust Devil was not a happy bull. I climbed up on the rails behind Book and fired off a string of, "Have you lost your mind!?" questions to which she paid me no mind. She had the rope wrapped tightly around one of her buckskin gloves and stared straight ahead. Several times the mighty bull tried to bust through the corral boards. He heaved up to try and claw his way out before they opened the gate nearly causing my heart to leap out of my chest. He slammed his horns on a board they slid in to keep his head down. I was sure that this was the last time I would see my good friend and riding partner.

The chute burst open and so did The Dirt Devil. He churned and twisted his way around the fence while Book hung on with one hand. To this day I don't remember even taking a breath. Time slowed down and the sound of the crowd faded. I could see the hats waving and clapping but the only sound I heard was that bull snorting and spitting and my heart beating like a jack rabbits. Try as he might, he could not shake Book off his back.

Finally tired out, he just stopped in the middle of the ring with his hooves spread apart. The dust settled and so did the roar of the crowd. There was a silence from the fences; everyone was holding their breath in an amazed hush. The great bull stood heaving and blowing steam out of his nostrils. People from the streets ran to see what had happened. Book untied her hand, stood up, and as graceful as a bird, jumped down, waved to us and headed toward the men with the money. Halfway across the dirt, she picked up a stick she found on the ground and walked back toward the bull. She whacked the bull's shoulder with the stick and walked away. Somewhere in the crowd and in the hills a few whoops could be heard. They could have only come from the unseen Indians that were surely watching.

We walked away from the stunned crowd counting out about twenty U.S. dollars, which we all agreed was well earned under the circumstances. We were sure that those cowboys never counted on paying off the prize money for their unridable animal that day or any other. What they also hadn't counted on is our guns trained in their general direction if they didn't ante up. I'm sure that no one ever heard of a time when an Indian had counted coup on a bull either. We set out to find our mares where the horses where being sold.

*

He had been tracking the group for days now. He almost killed the screaming woman but that would have been too easy. It was more fun to see her run around the flames to see if they burned her. There was no time to stay. Better to keep following and wait for his chance to catch the others which would be soon enough. He didn't like towns. Too many eyes and too much noise. The shadows and hills would have to keep him company for now. Then again, maybe one of his victims would come to him?

*

There was a man who had Dutch ovens buried partway into the ground with burning coals all around. The one he opened with an iron hook let out the most appealing smell and swirling steam that it made everyone within a mile water at the mouth. He was scooping meat out and served it up with bread. We were standing in a long line with so many other hungry customers. We soon overheard a conversation about a young Mexican who was said to have some of the best horses but would not sell to anyone who had inquired of him yet. We all decided after we ate to take a walk over to get a look at his animals and to see if the reports were true.

D let a low whistle out between her teeth when the Mexican with the horses came into view. "God amighty! I don't know whether I'm whistlin' at the horses or that man!"

The man was surely one of the best looking people we had ever seen. He sported tanned skin, thick wavy hair and a trimmed mustache.

Keys came up along side me and nodded her head. "Those there are what we need my friends. Spanish mares. I have to agree with your taste D, would you take a look at who's holding them."

We agreed to let Keys have a go with the negotiation since she spoke the best of the group. The man was soon shaking his head at her. His eyes were locked on Lupé the whole time. Keys walked back across the street and relayed his words to us. She had a little smile on her lips and a little flush to her cheeks as she looked from each one till she landed on Lupé. "He won't talk to anyone but you. Make it count."

As we watched from across the street, Lupé gave a determined march toward the man. She balled her fists and slammed them into her hips. As he began to talk, his eyes moved up and down over her outfit.

One thing you have to know is at that time men's pants on women were not smiled at in most situations. Sure, they were practical but were all the same frowned on. Who in Pike's name wanted to tramp around the ranch fightin' a skirt? For those brave one's who put pants on, nasty things were said or just plain made up. Book and I did well cuz we passed as boys but there was no hiding *some* curves from any right-minded male, if you know what I'm sayin'. We rode through and mostly passed off huffs from the bonnet wearers. We were doing what we had to.

As I was thinking, I noticed that Lupé's hand was coming up in a slap motion. Something about what the man was saying was making her mad. D leaned in and whispered in my ear. "If that knife-totin hothead ruins this deal for us, I'll kill her dead myself!"

Just as Lupé was going to put the slap on, the man grabbed her wrist and grinned widely. They stared at each other that way for a long minute to see if the other would back down. Finally, Lupé dropped her hand and stomped back in our direction.

"He say he remembers me from my village. He say he might sell horses to my pardners and take me back with him. He wants to talk with this little gringo cowboy." She threw her thumb in my general direction. "His name eez Levi, Levi Aguillaro."

Thing is, I was nearly all up on the prospect of killin' two birds at once. I could get rid of this troublesome girl and get us some fine horses in one shot. All was good in my mind until I looked over to see Book give me a sour stare. She must have seen the wheels turning in my head from a mile away. I figured I better just see what he had in mind first so I lit out in his direction.

"Thing is Levi, Lupé there is dead set on independent living. I know good horses when I see um but with the first thing in mind, I can't see how we can both come out of this deal clean."

Heads turned around town as our group passed by and when we stopped for supplies. We soon headed over the hills toward the Flying Bird with our little outfit. It included two boys, three women in pants, and a string of the prettiest Spanish-bred mares you ever did see. I still made Lupé ride point though.

One thing I did not share with the group was the deal breaker I made with Levi. I told him where the ranch was. I also gave him a personal invitation to visit as he pleased to pick out some of the new stock we would have on hand. I'm dead sure that Lupé being there might have swayed his decision. I'm also sure that Book was wondering why I couldn't wipe the stupid grin off my face for miles out of town.

25

We were double careful on the trip back. There were more than a few less-than-honest types who figured a few women and some boys with better than nice horses were an easy mark. We camped, but kept moving, took no help from passers-by, and we kept our guns close. More than once we saw shadows moving in the night. We kept our eyes on our horses to alert us of danger. If you wanted to know what was going on past what you could see or hear, your best bet was to watch your horse who could sense trouble in almost any situation.

At night watch we took turns and sent two out at a time. The last night D and Lupé were on watch. After that night D got real quiet and was not the same for the rest of the trip. We could not drag the details out of her. We turned to Lupé who told us that a mare had gotten loose and D went out after the horse into the trees. She came back a while after with the horse but said nothing for the rest of the watch.

The troubled mood of our outfit lightened up when we came to the hill that led to the valley of the ranch. We could see smoke trailing out of the chimney and big old Chop outside cutting wood. The fencing was finished and the outbuildings too. I can tell you, I was never in my life so glad to see the big red head of the Colonel as she marched out to check us over while we herded our new mares into the corral of their new home.

Everyone went in to clean up and talk about our adventures except Chop and me who were unsaddling the horses. I took The Red aside for a bit of deep conversation. "Look here old friend. Since we seem to be passin' out second chances round here, I reckon you should be in on the deal. Make it count!" I slapped him on the behind and off he went like a Roman fighter into the Coliseum. What? My ma read me some books.

"Leon, my good man, I'd eat a dern cat if you said you cooked one up about now." We smiled at each other and headed in with the rest.

*

"I'm tellin' ya right about now that your gonna' spill what you know or I'll pull this trigger and I won't miss!"

The Colonel raced up and put herself between D and myself which was a pretty brave move considering the gun I was waving in her face. Book had gone missing and it was past nightfall which wasn't like her. It for sure meant trouble. It was a couple of days since we got back from the sale and Book had been gone a whole day. D hadn't said a word as the day drug on. She just sulked around the ranch like a whipped dog. I was bordering on panic and needed answers fast. This wasn't like Book at all to leave and not give word. The Colonel broke in and pushed my gun down as she spoke to D.

"Were here girl. If you have something to tell us, your word is safe. No harm will come from it. Best to have out with it now."

D looked around the group and took a deep breath. Her lip shivered and her eyes filled up and I thought -oh God here it comes.

"There was a monster in the woods that night. The night on my watch. I went in after that mare. Branches were hittin' my face in the dark and next I know he had me. His big, black hands around my throat squeezin' me close with his stunk up breath in my face. It smelled like dead blood! He said I was not one of the ones he was lookin' for but if I told, he would come for me in the night. He told me he would cut me open so my guts would come spillin' out!"

She broke into a sorry sob and the Colonel wrapped her up in one of her arms. As she did, there was a shuffle of four little feet coming up behind the Colonel. With wide, teary eyes, the red heads told about how one of them had seen Book heading out in the early morning toward the barn with a "dark man."

I lit out for my horse, leaving the others behind. Keys took a grab for my shirt. I wheeled around with a fierce look on my face that made her take a step back. She yelled in my direction. "Look here! Ya'll don't know what has happened! Ya'll can't just go riding off into the night alone, with no help against this, this dark monster person!"

I turned to face the rest of them. "Say it! You all are sure as hell thinking it! You've passed it around in your little *circle*! You've heard the stories about me from your *customers*! I got no one now! If that Razorface killer wants me he can have me! Book was the best of us all I tell ya and she had no part in this mess!"

The Colonel stepped forward, "I've known many young ladies in my time. I reckon you are a hundred proof right about Talking Book but don't you sell yourself too cheap. You have been a great help to us all here and we are better off for it. You come back to us safe you hear. You and yer good friend Book. You got family at the Flying Bird Ranch."

I rode out into the darkness in search of my friend and partner with a heavy heart. I figured that if anything happened to her, I was to blame and I wasn't of a mind to go on without her.

26

"Follow closely now Abel. This is it, I can feel it. If we make a wrong move, they'll be more bodies to bury. Then we may as well add mine because if we lose um, I don't know if I can live with that."

Let's just say that old Abel stuck like glue. The prospect of hunting Razorface alone did not seem appealing, any way you cut it.

*

I got myself lured by the glow of the fire. There seemed to be some movement that I couldn't make out. The Red was nearly jumping out from under me. He was huffing and puffing with his ears swirling every which way. I could almost feel his heart beating through the saddle as I gripped my gun with white knuckles ignoring every warning sign. It was then my worst possible fears came to life. In the firelight I could see my friend lashed to two x-shaped logs of wood. Her eyes were closed and I could not tell if she was dead or alive. This sight took me straight back to that shack where we first met. The same old anger swept upon me like a flooded river out of control. I dropped my guard and rushed in. I saw a white light flash across my eye and I was yanked clean from my horse. Everything went dark.

The muscles in my eye tried to pry open my lid on the side of my face that took the hit. Soon, I wished I couldn't see at all. I had no idea how much time had passed. My eyes were blurry but I could see shadows' dancing round and round the fire with sparks floating up through the trees above. I was tied up like my friend on the same kind of crossed logs with the ropes cutting into my wrists.

My horse was nowhere in sight but what I could see was the most devilish man I had ever seen in my life. Just the feeling he gave off made my skin start to crawl all over. On his body were clothes blackened and stinking of death. I could make out that there were stains all on the fronts of his pant legs that he kept rubbing up and down with his hands. His almost toothless grin started toward me. I could just make out his greasy black hair and those X marks just above his eyes. I knew then that this was it. There was nothing I could do or say to get us out of this mess. My useless life had come to this. I didn't even have my guns. But Book, she didn't deserve to go this way. She believed in...

"Weeeelll now. Lookie heeere. Welcome to our little fiesta. Happy to have you join us. I have a place for your friend right heeere" He tapped the X's on his head.

It was the same voice I had heard in my room that night at the ranch. It was the same voice I heard in my nightmares for as long as I could remember. It was the same voice I heard when my pa beat the life out of us. It was the voice I heard that kept me running and killing too. It was the voice of death.

"I beet you taste reel niiice. Like a rabbit, eh?"

I looked over to Book and thought I saw her lips move a little but her eyes were still closed. They suddenly snapped open and she stared out into the dark at nothing. I thought maybe she finally chipped in her soul to Heaven. This gave me a thought and I did something that I never would have done before I met Book.

"Hello. I know...we both kinda know I brought this on myself, but Book here, she believes in you. She don't deserve this. I reckon we could use a little help right about now."

Monster X Face thought I was talking to him. He came out with a jagged knife that looked like it could cut down a tree and started singing a little tune.

"Buuzz buzzzz. Can you hear those buzzards bu.....?"

His little song was brought up short as a strip of rawhide swung high out of the trees and circled his neck. The last thing I saw was his eyes bugging out as he was whipped backwards through the air and disappeared into the darkness.

*

Boots had tracked a killer for miles untold. He had spent sleepless nights and bone rattling days in his saddle. He had endured endless conversations with his partner and talked strategies with the local law across more than one state line. He had endured the messy business of cutting down victims, digging graves, and hearing the cries of those left behind. All of these things added up prepared him for the decision he made that last dark night in the woods.

That night a small band of warriors floated silently by him with the killer lashed to the back of a war pony. They knew each was there, just like the split-second bond that brought them together against a common enemy. He reined his horse and rode away in the opposite direction. He would later write in his report to the Judge that he had found the body of the killer lashed to an X-shaped form and mutilated beyond recognition, except for the X-shaped marks running across his forehead. Justice served.

*

We were left with the crackle of the fire and sparks floating up and up. Then, out of the blackness came a group of painted warriors. I have never seen anything so fearsome and beautiful all at the same time. The largest one who seemed to be in charge spoke to Book in their language and she answered back.

The next thing I knew, we were being led into the night on our own horses. I was still struck silent by the shock of it all, glad to be alive and in the saddle riding next to Book.

The sun had made a break over the hills when we rode into camp. I had nodded off in the saddle and woke up with a pounding in my head and the shape of Indian tee pees in the distance. My heart was beating like mad. I looked around wildly for Book who had her chin held high and staring straight ahead with a serious face. Seeing her gave me comfort and I tried not to look as scared as I felt.

Every person in the camp seemed to gather around us as we were brought to a stop in front of a beautifully painted tee pee. One of the warriors spoke and the flap was drawn back from the inside with an extra large brown hand. Out popped a tall black hat with an eagle feather stuck to one side. His deerskin shirt fringe swayed back and forth with many colored beads and metal bells that seemed to be made out of tin can lids, shining when they caught the light. He had long, shiny black hair that was slicked back under his hat so I could see his eyes perfectly. They were a deep brown-black with the sunrise coming up behind them. The lashes were the wings of a great black bird. They were the eyes of Talking Book.

*

We were brought into the tee pee and I looked back to see my horse being admired by a group of young men surrounding him. A tee pee inside is much bigger than you might think. There was a pit for fire in the middle and comfortable buffalo skins laid out for sitting and sleeping. Things hung here and there from the wood poles. There was talking between the Chief and Book going on with my name thrown out here and there. I was taking it all in when my eyes locked on a picture that was hung up for decoration. It was of a Mexican man with an extra large mustache that I knew all to well. Next to the picture was a stack of used-up pomade cans.

She made an introduction, "Cisco Peach, my father, Chief Medicine Hair."

The chief stepped in front of me and broke into a wide grin. He led me to the stack of hair pomade cans and pointed. He looked toward Book with a proud expression, and then nodded his head with approval. She looked at me with a smirk. "He uses your hair pomade."

She disappeared out of the flap and reappeared with an armful of new Cisco Peach pomade cans that she unpacked from her saddlebag.

"We bought these at the Stock Sale. We were going to have a little fun and put them in your room. I think they might be of better use to us here. I told him that we needed protection for the Flying Bird as a gift in return."

The chief's face lit up when he spotted the cans. His bet had finally paid off. His girl had returned with the goods.

*

We rode off with our own horses, full bellies, and an escort of warriors who disappeared into the trees as we came to the hill that overlooked the valley of the Flying Bird Ranch.

I sat there on The Red thinking on all we had done and had yet to do. We could just turn and keep riding the trail. We were free of the killer and if the law were coming, it would have come down on us already. We sat there overlooking the valley and I knew that Book could see the wheels turning. If she had concern, it didn't show. I took a deep breath and gave my horse a kick. I didn't look back but I knew she had a smile at the corner of her lips.

That night we all sat at the table together and Book said her thanks over the meal. I can tell you she was mighty shocked when she ended her prayer and I finished it with an "Amen." I owed Him one after all.

Afterwords...

A few winters had come and gone and spring was here again. With it brought another fine crop of Flying Bird foals. We saw shadows of warriors now and again but we never had one horse go missing since our visit with Chief Medicine Hair. Book kept up her end of the bargain and sent a can or two over to the chief on a regular basis. Word spread of our venture and our fine stock. We had plenty of business coming in; we even had a few buyers from the southern states. Keys joked that if her father ever were to show his face, prices would more than triple just for him.

Book was worth her weight in gold when it came to breaking and training and we all became fast students of the now famous Indian bull rider. D was the best at breaking, being full of gun powder herself. She even went on to become quite the fierce bronc rider. She would travel with the Wild West shows, only to ride over the hill and back home to the ranch to tell us her tales.

"That Buffalo Bill ain't all what he puts on but he's good to his girls." She'd say. "Hey Cisco, why don't you come with me on the next run? You need to meet this Little Sure Shot Miss Annie Oakley. God amighty! That girl can shoot!"

The Colonel made good with her business sense and the ranch ran like a finely made time piece. More than once a girl would show up on our door step hoping to escape the torments of the old "life." The ones that stayed, we put to work and the ones that didn't, we let go. Everyone that left went away with a full belly and the best we could give in the way of advice. Somehow we all knew that we were running more than a horse outfit. Even the two red-headed twins had become good little riders and grew like weeds. They still didn't talk much but I got the shock of my life one day when one smiled and put her thin arms around my waist for a quick hug.

I spent my days running the ranch with the other "hands" and being glad to have found a home at last. I still rode out with my good friend Book a time or two. We would talk of our adventures and times to come. Evenings came and the Colonel and myself would have our smoke time on the front porch where it all began.

One evening a rider was coming down over the hill that I immediately recognized as one Levi Aguillaro. That same stupid grin was back on my face. I was about to kill the second bird with one stone. So much for Lupé. I was bettin' on the fact that he would not give up on taking her with him. Did I mention that his mother had named him after a pair of men's mining pants?